Praise for Melody Carlson

"This satisfying Christmas novel will find year-round fans."

"Carlson puts a charming, Christmassy spin on a rags-to-royalty Cinderella story. Readers will cheer on her spunky, earnest heroine."

"Carlson's latest impeccably written inspirational romance is wholesome holiday fun for readers who like their romances dressed up with a bit of fairy-tale glitz and glam."

"*A Quilt for Christmas* brings out all of the feels."

"Carlson adds emotional depth with moments of humor and enduring faith in the face of loss. This is sure to tug on readers' heartstrings."

"Equally hilarious and heartrending, Carlson's novel draws on her own experience as a caregiver to provide a devastatingly real novel of deep, quiet faith in the face of a family's worst fear."

Once Upon a
CHRISTMAS
CAROL

Books by Melody Carlson

Christmas at Harrington's
The Christmas Shoppe
The Joy of Christmas
The Treasure of Christmas
The Christmas Pony
A Simple Christmas Wish
The Christmas Cat
The Christmas Joy Ride
The Christmas Angel Project
The Christmas Blessing
A Christmas by the Sea
Christmas in Winter Hill
The Christmas Swap
A Christmas in the Alps
A Quilt for Christmas
A Royal Christmas
The Christmas Tree Farm
Once Upon a Christmas Carol

Once Upon a
CHRISTMAS CAROL

A Christmas Novella

MELODY CARLSON

Revell

a division of Baker Publishing Group
Grand Rapids, Michigan

© 2025 by Carlson Management Company

Published by Revell
a division of Baker Publishing Group
Grand Rapids, Michigan
RevellBooks.com

Printed in the United States of America

Library of Congress Cataloging-in-Publication Data
Names: Carlson, Melody, author.
Title: Once upon a Christmas carol : a Christmas novella / Melody Carlson.
Description: Grand Rapids, Michigan : Revell, a division of Baker Publishing Group, 2025.
Identifiers: LCCN 2024053715 | ISBN 9780800744731 (cloth) | ISBN 9781493451401 (ebook)
Subjects: LCGFT: Christmas fiction. | Romance fiction. | Novels.
Classification: LCC PS3553.A73257 O527 2025 | DDC 813/.54—dc23/eng/20250122
LC record available at https://lccn.loc.gov/2024053715

This book is a work of fiction. Names, characters, places, and incidents are the product of the author's imagination or are used fictitiously. Any resemblance to actual events, locales, or persons, living or dead, is coincidental.

Jacket illustration: Nate Eidenberger
Jacket design: Laura Klynstra

Baker Publishing Group publications use paper produced from sustainable forestry practices and postconsumer waste whenever possible.

25 26 27 28 29 30 31   7 6 5 4 3 2 1

N
o one knew that Carol Langstrom hated Christmas. Okay, *hate* was a strong word, but thanks to her parents' dysfunctional relationship during her childhood—particularly whenever the holidays came around—she would nearly break out into hives at the sound of "Jingle Bells." One year she had even complained to a big-box store manager when she saw a display of artificial trees before Halloween. And those obnoxious "have a perfect Christmas" online pop-up ads nearly drove her to distraction. Some people counted the days until Christmas, but her countdown went until December 26 because she couldn't wait until Christmas was over and done with.

As an employee of a home-staging firm that spent most of the year getting expensive houses ready to sell but caved to focus on holiday decor in late October, the months following Halloween were something to endure and escape. Carol knew the layout of the holiday section of their warehouse by heart and even dreamed about its colorful contents sometimes. Her boss's love of everything Christmas had begun years ago. Marsha Forrester had collected dedicated clientele along with faux life-sized reindeer, enormous pine-scented artificial trees, five-foot-tall nutcrackers, and enough realistic-looking elves to fill a shelter for unemployed height-challenged holiday workers.

Early on, Carol learned to conceal her yuletide phobia when the calendar turned to November. From that day on, Divine Design seemed to go into hypermode, concocting everyone's dream Christmas. Well, not everyone. Just the well-heeled, self-obsessed, somewhat overindulgent, and entitled clients. All of whom seemed to have Divine Design on speed dial and were equally determined to outdo their neighbors and friends with the very latest in "festive yet tasteful" holiday decor. People, in her undisclosed opinion, had too much time and money on their hands. Of course, she kept her personal feelings toward them and Christmas to herself. After all, she was a working girl.

"Carol," Marsha Forrester said urgently over the phone. "Did you drop the new wreaths at the Barstrums' yet?"

Carol could tell by the sharp tone that her normally cool and controlled boss was even more stressed than she sounded right now.

"Yes," Carol answered. "I removed the dried ones and hung the fresh wreaths myself. But if Mrs. Barstrum had simply spritzed the originals with the bottle of water I left for her, or asked her housekeeper to do it, they would've been fine. The sun just beats down on that southern exposure—"

"Yes, yes, I know," Marsha said, cutting her off. "And I did remind her that our faux wreaths are even prettier than fresh ones, not to mention reusable, but she insists on the real thing."

"Right." Carol slid her black carry-on bag into the back seat of her Uber and listened impatiently as Marsha droned on about how they might be better off by letting some clients go next year.

"Just the difficult ones, of course."

"The holidays have gotten super busy for us." Carol peered at the darkening sky. "Anything else?"

"I suppose you're on your way to the airport by now?" Marsha sounded a little wistful. "Off to your sunny destination. I'll admit your plan sounded a bit harebrained at first—I mean,

Christmas in the Bahamas of all places—but it's suddenly rather appealing."

"Especially with this storm coming." Carol slid in, closed the car door, and leaned back. "Seattle's supposed to be inundated with a deluge by tomorrow."

"Someone must've been dreaming of a *wet* Christmas here." Marsha laughed without sounding particularly jolly. "Well, think of me while you're down there working on your tan."

"I'll send you pics," Carol promised. "Have a good Christmas, Marsha."

"You too, Carol. Oh, by the way, have a good birthday too. I always forget that you share your birthday with Jesus. My little Christmas Carol." She chuckled like this was a new joke and not something Carol had heard her entire life. "And I believe this year is a big one for you too." Her laughter had a sharpness to it. "But don't worry, honey, today's forty is yesterday's thirty. Just wait until you hit the big 6-0 like me next spring. Now that's getting serious."

"Oh, Marsha, you're so youthful for your age," Carol reassured her egotistical boss, reminding her that age was just a number as the Uber driver expertly navigated the late-day city traffic toward SeaTac. But even as she smoothed Marsha's vain feathers, her mind wandered to how she was what some would call middle-aged yet was still stuck in the single lane.

"Well, I must go. Warren is here to take me to dinner." The sound of air kisses came over the phone and then the call ended. Carol slid her phone into her purse and wondered if it was fair to call forty middle-aged. Sure, if one only lived to eighty that would be true. But weren't people supposed to live longer these days? Still . . .

Carol was good at faking a lot of things. Like not despising Christmas, or that cream-colored sofas were sensible for a client with two ill-mannered doodle dogs and an elderly, incontinent cat. She could even pretend that she loved her "career in design," which was mostly staging homes for realtors once the holidays were behind them. She could even feign how lovely it was living alone and being "independent" and act like remaining single was her personal preference.

But with each passing year spent alone, it seemed to matter a bit more. Just not enough for her to settle down. And that was exactly what she'd be doing if she got seriously involved with any of the men who had pursued her—*settling*. And that did not sit well with her. Of course, even if she did meet Mr. Right, perhaps in the Bahamas, would she even know it? Besides, didn't she always tell her girlfriends, the ones who were also still looking, that Mr. Right was a mere figment in fairy tales and Hallmark movies?

By the time her driver pulled into the Delta terminal, the rain was pelting sideways in enormous droplets. She would not miss this a bit! She thanked the driver, gathered her bag, and was relieved to see that she still had ample time to make it through security and grab a bite. Feeling strangely out of place in her summery garb and sandals when everyone else sported parkas and slickers and winter hats and scarves, she made her way to her gate. After overhearing passenger chatter in TSA about a storm blustering on the Atlantic and the possibility of cancelations, she wanted to ensure her direct flight to Miami wasn't affected.

To her relief her flight wasn't even delayed. Imagining a nasty nor'easter pounding into the Eastern seaboard, not down South where she was headed, she felt relatively reassured as she waited for a seat in a crowded café. She should be in Nassau by midday tomorrow, basking in the sun with all thoughts of Christmas blown away by this inconvenient winter storm. She almost felt sorry for the passengers whose journeys might be rocked by Mother Nature's Christmas present. Almost.

As she dined on a chef salad and a glass of white wine, she began to truly relax for the first time in weeks. She had this vacation in the bag. Sure, her father and stepmother were miffed that she wasn't joining them for Christmas. They wondered why she wasn't dying to visit them in their fabulous estate in British Columbia, like she usually did. But she'd never really bonded with Dad's new wife and never really felt at home in their "perfect" house. Her stepmom Barb had bought it with her divorce settlements, then furnished it with only the "best of the best."

It made no difference that Carol's parents had been apart for almost thirty years now, that her mom had left Dad for another man, or that their marriage had been a disaster for as long as Carol could remember . . . Something about their miserable break had always left Carol feeling more broken than ever during the holidays. Probably because as a child that's when she always felt torn down the middle.

Still, like so many other things, she'd learned to cleverly conceal this childish angst beneath a veneer of togetherness and sophisticated nonchalance. She rationalized that her "selfless" rationale was to protect those around her. She'd spare them from seeing her old wounds or sensing her pain. Especially during the holidays. But she knew that wasn't wholly true . . . her pride was wrapped up in the facade too.

The alarm on her phone chimed, jarring her back to reality. It was time to head to her gate for boarding. Her check prepaid, she only needed to grab her lightweight carry-on and hurry down the bustling terminal. With no coat or hat or miscellaneous travel gear to wrestle with, she hurried past an artificial Christmas tree, then, with the tinny sound of "Twelve Days of Christmas" grating on her ears like a dentist's drill, she paused to let a woman burdened with cumbersome luggage and two small children go past her.

Carol smiled pleasantly at them, winking at the little boy with the chocolate-smudged face. The kids were cute, but Carol was mostly smiling at how lightly she had been able to pack. It was unusual for a person who liked to be prepared for everything when she traveled, but Carol never had much use for summer clothes in Seattle. Plus, bringing little gave her a good excuse to peruse shops in Nassau. She'd heard it was a trendy place. As she turned toward her gate, she couldn't help but observe even more anxious faces, which drew her attention to the gate signs. Red streaks across the screens told her there'd been numerous delays and several cancelations. Hers was one of the few flights with no changes. She sighed in relief, even though she felt for the many now-stranded travelers all around her. But traveling during the holidays was like that. You had to roll with the punches, right?

She kept moving forward until she reached her gate, where passengers were already lined up. Like her, most were dressed for warm weather and in good spirits. Jokes were made about how they were all escaping the big winter storm. Before long, they were loaded on, buckled in, and preparing for takeoff. She stared out the window at the darkened skies as they taxied. The illuminated runways were being pounded with sheets of rain. Good riddance, Seattle, see you next year!

No time was wasted on the soggy runway, but shortly after takeoff they were hit with strong turbulence. Yet no one seemed concerned. Passengers remained in good spirits, making light of the bouncy ride, and flight attendants assured everyone they'd soon be out of it and drinks would be served.

Not generally a fan of air travel, Carol attempted to ignore the bumpiness, focusing instead on the beach read she'd loaded onto her Kindle that morning. She preferred a "real" book in her hands and planned to get something good at the resort, but she had been determined to travel light, so this would do for now. After a while, the flight smoothed out and Carol closed her eyes and, thanks to her earlier glass of pinot gris, managed to fall asleep.

But she woke to a violently jolting plane and the pilot's calm but serious voice on the intercom system. "We're forced to make an unscheduled stop in Grand Rapids." He cleared his throat. "This is due to a development of multiple tornadoes down south."

"Tornadoes?" echoed the man behind Carol.

"Grand Rapids?" the older woman at her side exclaimed. "Why on earth are we going there?"

"Probably because they're not having tornadoes in Michigan," the man in the aisle seat said. "Don't get yourself all worked up, Helen. We'll catch another flight when the weather clears."

"How long will *that* take?" she demanded.

"Do I look like a weatherman?" he growled back.

"Well, you're the one who insisted we needed to take this trip at Christmastime," she shot back. "I told you it was a ridiculous idea." And on they bickered, back and forth. Meanwhile, the whole atmosphere of the plane followed their lead. The previously cheery crowd began to groan and complain as frustrated flight attendants attempted to calm everyone.

"It's just a temporary inconvenience," the flight attendant patiently told the feuding couple. "You'll get connected to other flights in the terminal. It might take some doing, but you'll reach your final destination. The storm won't last forever."

By the time Carol rolled her "lightweight" carry-on through the crowded Gerald R. Ford International Airport, it was feeling heavier. Outside, illuminated by airport lights, snow was starting to fly, and inside, all the TVs were tuned to news and weather stations as anchors reported that several major storm fronts had converged on the Eastern seaboard from Maine to Florida and were wreaking havoc on air travel. As she walked through, trying to decide what to do now, Carol noticed how every gate was bearing the dreaded "canceled" signs. Instead of looking like a terminal, the place resembled a messy campground with people and bags piling up everywhere.

Although she knew it was probably pointless, Carol joined a herd of other disgruntled travelers who were lined up in front of Delta's information counter, staffed by a single clerk. When Carol's turn finally came, she could see the weary young woman had memorized her spiel and was politely reciting the same message she'd given the rest.

"We're so sorry for your inconvenience. It's unlikely that any flights will go out before midday tomorrow, but we do expect this storm to pass by then. We suggest you wait it out in an airport hotel and contact us later for more flight information.

Probably by morning." The clerk smiled stiffly and handed Carol a list of airline numbers and domains as well as the names of some local hotels. "Have a good day."

Carol thanked her and, resisting the urge to point out it was nighttime, reached for her phone. After calling several of the nearby hotels, where she either got a busy signal or a recording saying there were no vacancies, she gave up. Checking the time, she realized that here in the eastern portion of the country, morning was just a few hours away. Why not simply camp out in the airport and be first in line for morning flights? And like scores of other weary travelers hoping to get comfy, she found a corner in a less-crowded gate, secured a seat near the window, and returned to her beach read, using her carry-on as a footstool. It helped a little, but it wasn't like stretching out on a sunny Bahamian beach without a care in the world . . . Hopefully by tomorrow.

The book failed to transport her, and out the nearby window, the winter sky remained dark, snow continued to fall, and morning felt like it had been abducted by some evil force. Carol's back throbbed from the hard seat, and her sandaled feet felt like swollen ice cubes. To thaw them and get some blood flowing, she found a kiosk with stale coffee and walked around the terminal, sipping and watching for an agent to come and occupy the ticket counter where a few disgruntled travelers were already clustered like vultures.

Finally, a dull gray light began to illuminate one of the big windows. Even then the only thing really visible was a nearby runway blanketed in snow with even more blowing down in what appeared to be nearly whiteout conditions. A chill ran through Carol as she looked out on the scene.

After getting a fresher cup of coffee, she stood with a crowd gathered around the TVs listening as newscasters called this "the storm of the century," which sounded more unbelievable each time they said it. Hadn't they been saying that for years now? But clearly no flights would depart this airport anytime soon. Feeling totally discombobulated, Carol sat down to ponder her situation. Getting a hotel seemed like an impossible dream but she tried anyway, hoping some travelers might've checked out in hopes of finding flights.

After many fruitless calls, she suddenly recalled her mom had an older sister who lived somewhere in Michigan. Although her mother and aunt were estranged, Carol remembered how this aunt used to send Christmas cards. Greetings her mom tossed in the trash, sometimes unopened, along with some harsh muttered words. For as long as Carol could remember, her mom had harbored a boatload of anger and resentment toward her older sister, but she'd always refused to divulge her reasons. Still, if Carol had a relative living nearby, perhaps they'd have a spare bed. Anything was better than another night trying to sleep in an uncomfortable chair among strangers.

Of course, Michigan was a large state, and it was very possible this aunt lived too far away. Or that she'd moved. And even if her home was nearby, could Carol possibly impose on someone she'd never met? Just until flights resumed? She wondered how old this aunt might be. Mom used to say that Maria helped raise her, but Mom was in her mid-sixties. Her sister might be ancient, or she could have passed on. And road travel in this weather could be too perilous for an elderly woman. Besides that, what about the sisterly dispute? Of course, that was a long time ago, and Carol was well aware that Mom could hold grudges. Maybe she'd brought this estrangement on herself . . . Or this older sister could be a real witch.

Feeling she had little to lose, Carol picked up her phone, which was in desperate need of a charge. She hadn't spoken to her mother in ages. They rarely talked anymore, not even at Christmastime. Did she really want to deal with her now? It was possible her mother's number had changed. That had happened before. But feeling desperate and hopeless, she gave it a try. To her surprise, her mom answered right away in her deep, raspy voice. "Mom, uh, is that you?" Carol suddenly felt tongue-tied.

"Carol Louise!" Mom said eagerly. "I was just thinking of you last night. How serendipitous that you should call. How are you doing, darling?"

"Well, not so good actually." Carol gave a quick lowdown on her unraveling travel plans. "So I'm kind of stuck in Grand Rapids of all places."

"That explains why you're calling so early. But believe it or not, I was actually awake."

"Sorry. I forgot the time difference."

"That's okay. I was just sitting out here on the patio in the moonlight having me a smoke. Please, no lectures. But, good grief, if you have to be stuck somewhere, why Grand Rapids? Isn't that in the northeast somewhere?"

"It's in Michigan. And it wasn't exactly my choice to get stuck here." Carol tried to keep exasperation from her voice. After all, her mom was being surprisingly friendly.

"Too bad you didn't get laid over down here in Phoenix. We're having a beautiful weather, and—"

"I'm glad to hear it," Carol interrupted. Her mom could go on and on about trivial matters when she was in the mood, which she seemed to be now. "I actually called because I think I remember you mentioned having a sister up here in Michigan."

"Oh, yeah, Maria." Her tone grew sharper. "I suppose she still lives up there. She's been there forever."

"You don't happen to have her phone number, do you?"

"Are you kidding?" Her laugh sounded more like a cackle, followed by a smoker's cough. "Sorry, sweetie, but Maria and I aren't exactly on speaking terms."

"Right." Carol frowned. "What about her full name? Or her husband's name. Maybe I could look them up."

"Good grief. Why would you do that?"

"Because half the holiday travelers are stranded here, there are no hotel vacancies, and I just spent the night in the airport and am tired."

"Oh, well then, I suppose any port in a storm." She humphed. "Well, her name is Maria O'Harney. I remember the O'Harney name because she married an Irish man and Dad never forgave her for that."

"I see. And do you recall Mr. O'Harney's first name?"

"Ron? Tom? Don?" She paused. "Yes, that's it. Donald O'Harney."

"Great. Now do you happen to know where they live? Is it anywhere near Grand Rapids by any chance?"

"Really? You expect me to remember that too?" Another pause. "Well, I do recall he was a teacher in Grand Rapids, but that was eons ago." Mom hemmed and hawed. "You know, Maria used to send me Christmas cards. That is until Ed and me moved out here. She either quit sending them or the post office just don't forward them anymore. But seems I recall Dad saying that Donald gave up a perfectly good teaching job to buy a silly little farm in a one-horse town. Sounded like a dumb move to me."

"Do you have any idea what the town was called? That might help."

Mom started rattling some names off. "It had Creek or Springs or some kind of water word in it, but my memory is getting more and more like Swiss cheese these days. There's some holes." She laughed.

"Well, that might be enough to start a search. Thanks, Mom." Carol sighed. "It's not like I have many options anyway or anything else to do." She paused when her phone beeped. "I have to go before my cell battery gives out. "If I do find your sister, do you want me to tell her hello for you?"

Mom coughed loudly. "No thanks, sweetie. As far as I'm concerned, Maria is dead."

"Okay then." Carol took a deep breath. "I hope you and Ed have a good Christmas."

"You too, darling. Nice to hear your voice. Call me again and let me know how things turn out, okay?"

Carol agreed to do this but felt fairly certain she would "conveniently" forget. Hopefully she'd be so occupied with her Bahamian vacation by tomorrow, she'd be too busy to call anyone. That seemed a reasonable excuse.

After finding an unoccupied outlet, she plugged in her charger and started her search for small farm towns near Grand Rapids with a water word in the name. After trying Sugar Springs, she tried Venus Lake and then Miller's Creek and got lucky. A Donald and Maria O'Harney appeared to be residents with ages listed as mid-seventies. That seemed to fit. Encouraged by this, Carol even put the extra directory charge on her credit card in order to obtain their number and full address. And suddenly the phone was ringing . . . and ringing . . . and ringing. She checked the terminal clock overhead, worried perhaps she was calling too early. But it was after seven now, and if they were a farm family like Mom had said, they should be up.

"Hello?" an elderly female voice crackled over the phone.

"Hello?" Carol tried not to sound too desperate. "Is this the O'Harneys'?"

"Yes, and if you're trying to sell me something, you can just—"

"No, no, I'm sorry to disturb you, but I think you might be my aunt."

"That's just fine. Now, if you're a scammer, and you're about to tell me you're in jail and need bail money, you can go jump in a lake. I already got troubles aplenty, thank you very—"

"I'm really sorry to bother you." Carol couldn't help but smile. This woman had spirit. "But can you tell me, are you Maria? Is your maiden name Banducci?"

"Yes . . . ?" Her tone, still laced with suspicion, softened slightly.

"And is your younger sister Rosa Louise Banducci?"

The other end went silent.

"Hello?" Carol worried she'd lost the connection—or that the woman had hung up.

"Is this about Rosa?" Maria asked with quiet urgency. "Did something happen to her? Is she, is she . . . dead?"

"No, no, not at all. In fact, I just spoke with her. She's alive and well in Phoenix, Arizona. I'm her daughter, Carol Langstrom."

"You're Carol? Carol Louise? Goodness gracious . . . Well, I never."

"I'm not sure how close Miller's Creek is to Grand Rapids, but I'm on my way to the Bahamas for a vacation and got stuck at the airport. I really could use a shower . . . and a bed. Even for just a few hours if flights ever get going again today." Her nerves spiked at the silence on the other end. "I mean, if you have room."

"Of course. I have plenty of room." Maria paused. "But I'm not able to come get you."

Carol's heart sank. "I know this weather is atrocious. I didn't expect you to drive."

"Oh, it's not that. I drive in weather like this all the time. It's just that I can't right now. Not today anyway."

"I thought I could take an Uber?"

"A what?"

"A taxi. Do you think a taxi would go that far?"

"Oh, goodness, that'd cost a fortune, honey. No, don't do that. Tell you what, I'll send Victor for you. He owes me a favor since he'll be driving Don's old Chevy. I was about to call him just now anyway. Give me your number, and I'll call you right back if he can go fetch you. And even if he can't, we'll figure some way to get you out here."

Carol recited her number, then said goodbye and ended the call. After about five minutes, her phone chimed, and her aunt said to look for "an old red pickup with rails and a plow" and that Victor would be there in about an hour. "Due to the snow. Otherwise, it'd be half that time. But you gotta take it slower in the snow."

Carol thanked her and hung up, then wondered if this was a ridiculous plan. She looked around the still-crowded terminal, seeing weary travelers, most with dismal expressions as they looked at their phones. All gates still proclaimed that flights were canceled. Well, for better or worse, she would meet her aunt and uncle today. If nothing else, it should be interesting. Carol had never experienced much family growing up. Her dad had one younger brother who lived in eastern Washington. She'd met him and his relatively large family only a handful of times. As she recalled, his four kids were all very loud boys. Plus, they'd been quite a bit younger than her, and she'd never had much fun with them when they came to visit. She was always glad to see them loaded back up in their minivan heading for home.

After about forty minutes passed, she went down to the passenger pickup area and stared out the window. Still pondering over family and relatives, she wondered if she might have other cousins. If Maria and Don had kids, they'd most likely be older than Carol since it sounded like Maria was at least ten years older than Mom. Maybe Victor was their son, which would make him Carol's first cousin. Might be nice to have a cousin. She saw a red pickup pull up, but it was a newer model driven by a woman, and a man and teenager ran out to get inside. She kept her eye on the busy lanes of traffic and wondered what rails and a plow were, anyway? Was Victor driving a tractor?

She checked her phone to see that nearly an hour had passed. The blizzard was still raging. What if roads, like the runways, were closed and Victor wasn't able to get through? Would some-one let her know? She was about to call Maria back when she noticed an older pickup that, beneath its coat of snow, appeared red. A big thing on the front bumper was probably a snowplow and alongside the bed were wooden boards that resembled a fence. She figured those must be the plow and rails. This must be her cousin. Waving, she stepped outside, toting her carry-on with wind whipping at her flimsy, unbuttoned cardigan.

She shivered and attempted a feeble smile as a tall, lanky man dressed in a fleece-lined leather coat, blue jeans, and a cowboy hat hopped out and jogged around to meet her. "I'm Victor. You must be Carol. Let's get out of this pronto." Just as he reached for her carry-on, a strong gust of wind flipped his hat off his head. She reached up to grab it, but a thin leather strap beneath his chin kept it from taking flight. "Stampede strings," he said, winking. "Now get inside"—he yanked open the passenger door and practically shoved her in—"before you freeze your, uh, rear end off."

He slammed the door with a loud clang and swooped up her bag, easily tossing it into the pickup bed—right into a heap of snow. Then with his hat flapping in the wind behind him, he ran around to the driver's side and hopped in. As she watched him remove his hat, giving it a shake before hanging it on a gun rack behind him, she wanted to comment about how he'd buried her bag in the snow, but then she saw how cramped the cab was and kept silent. Her waterproof bag was probably snow-proof as well. Her feet felt icier than ever, but at least it was warm in here. Or warmer, at least. She shivered. Maybe calling it warm was an exaggeration.

"Here," he handed her a plaid wool blanket. "Put this around you." He shook his head. "Man, you sure don't know how to dress for weather, do you?"

"I wasn't planning on being in Michigan today," she replied a bit sharply.

"Obviously." He put the truck into gear and pulled out.

"I'm supposed to be in the Bahamas right now." She knew her tone was haughty, but she couldn't seem to stop herself.

"Well, someone must've got confused." He laughed.

She suspected he meant her but didn't see the humor in the situation. "My flight got redirected. But if I was in the Bahamas, I assure you I'd be quite comfortable. They happen to have a very warm climate down there. Unlike here."

"Well, you're not in the Bahamas. And any seasoned traveler flying in wintertime should be prepared for any kind of weather or possible layover. Neither are uncommon during the holidays."

As much as she tried, she couldn't think of the perfect smart aleck response to his derisive comment. And he was probably right. She should've been prepared. If any of the terminal shops had been open, she would've bought some warm socks and shoes and perhaps even some kind of jacket. But she decided not to pick a fight since her cousin was focused on driving—probably a good thing considering some of the mishaps she witnessed along the side of the road—and since he'd traveled a fair distance to get her. She wasn't sure if the cars she saw were abandoned or stranded or what, but a number of vehicles were partially buried in snow here and there. Conditions really were hazardous. Perhaps she'd have been safer at the airport after all, but it was too late for that now.

"I, uh, I assume you get weather like this a lot in Michigan?" she queried. "People are used to driving in it?"

"Not necessarily. I mean, the weather. Our winters can do just about anything from be unseasonably warm to something like this. It's not very predictable. At least not for the last five years or so. But the severity of this storm did catch some folks by surprise."

"Apparently." She pointed to a pair of cars that had clearly collided at an intersection up ahead. "I just figured people up here would know how to handle driving in snow better than this."

"They do handle it better when it's only snow, but this storm started with rain that turned to a sheet of ice and was then covered with snow. Have you ever driven on ice?"

She tried to remember. "I, uh, I don't think so. We really don't get too much ice in Seattle. And when we do, I stay home."

"You're from Seattle?"

"Yes. Didn't your mom ever mention that?"

"Not that I recall." As he waited for the light to change, he turned to look at her, a curious expression on his face. "Should she have?"

"I guess not." She pointed ahead. "The light's green."

"Thanks." He gently moved forward. She had to give him credit. He was a cautious driver. As he navigated the mostly empty city streets, finally turning off on a more rural sort of road, she studied him. He was definitely good-looking. With his thick, wavy hair and dark eyes, he appeared to take after the Italian side of the family. She'd only met her maternal grand-father once. She'd been four years old when Mom had taken her to visit Poppy Banducci, as Mom had told her to call him. They'd taken a train somewhere back East, but all Carol really remembered was a big, dirty city and having to climb stairs up to an apartment that was too hot and smelled strange. All to see the white-haired old man who never budged from his recliner, held an unlit pipe, and kept telling her to "speak up!"

She glanced at Victor again, wondering if he'd ever met Poppy Banducci. But unless she was mistaken, her cousin wasn't much older than her . . . or he was aging well. So his experience with Poppy, if he'd had any, was probably similar to hers. Even so, for the sake of conversation, she was about to ask when he spoke up.

"I was pretty surprised to hear Maria has a niece."

Carol felt her brows arch. "That's what you call her? Maria?"

He shrugged. "We're pretty informal around here. I could call her Mrs. O'Harney, but I doubt she'd like that much."

"No, I guess not. I just assumed you'd call her *Mom*. I tried calling my mom by her first name once when I was a teenager, because she was, well, let's just say she's never been terribly maternal. But when I called her Rosa, I thought she was going to knock me down."

He raised his brows. "Did your mom hit you?"

She couldn't help but chuckle. "No, but she had quite a temper."

He laughed. "My mom is hot-tempered too, but she mostly just yelled when I was a kid. I guess it comes with being Italian."

"That's what my dad used to say about my mom. Probably not very PC, but he called it her hot Italian blood. Her temper was one of the reasons they split. Just one of many."

"Your parents divorced?"

She nodded. "Yeah. I was just a kid so it was a long time ago. I don't think I was scarred too much by it." She forced a laugh. "I'm not seeing a therapist or anything."

"I'm sorry."

"That I'm not seeing a therapist?" she teased.

Now he laughed, making the edges of his eyes crinkle in an attractive way. Maybe he was older than she'd guessed. Well, if first impressions were true, and she knew from experience that a person could be fooled, Victor was a good guy. And perhaps this unplanned visit with relatives would turn out better than expected. Any port in a storm, right?

3

meant I was sorry that your parents split up," Victor clari-
fied as they came into a small town. Like everything else, the
quiet-looking main street was covered in snow. As she took
in what little she could see, she wondered how much farther
they had to go or how long this storm would last. But the flag
flapping by the post office was fully extended and whipping so
hard, she had no doubt it was still blowing out there.

Forcing herself to remember what their conversation was
about, she thanked him for his empathy. "My parents were
really better off after the divorce. Their fights were less toxic,
although I still found myself in the middle a good bit." She
sighed.

"Kids usually pay the highest price. A lot of my college
friends had divorced parents. Even as adults, it's not easy. And
yet about half of marriages fail."

"I sometimes think that's why so many people our age aren't
marrying. It's too risky."

"I suppose it is. For some folks, anyway."

"I'm guessing your parents have been together a long time."

"For sure. They'll hit the big fifty next year." He slowly shook
his head "Well, if Dad makes it that long."

"Oh, dear. Is he ill?"

"Alzheimer's. He's had it for a while, but the past year has been a little touch and go so you never know." He explained a bit more about his dad's medical issues.

"I'm sorry. Your poor mom. That must be hard on her." Carol was having serious regrets visiting her aunt and uncle now. Maybe it really was bad timing.

"That's why I moved home," he said. "I've been back a few years now to help out. Our farm isn't big, and we cut way back on livestock, but it still takes a fair amount of maintenance."

"Maybe this was a bad time for me to pop in unexpected." She suddenly imagined how overwhelmed her aunt could be feeling right now. Ailing husband, blizzard blowing, farm responsibilities, holidays . . . Why hadn't Carol thought this through better? She blamed it on a lack of sleep and cold feet. "Maria assured me she has room, but it sounds like she might have enough on her plate right—"

"Don't worry about Maria. She sounded excited to see you when she called." He frowned slightly. "Although she did mention bad timing. But I figured she meant with Christmas next week. Her decorations are always way over the top . . . and she's usually in charge of the town's Christmas Cotillion. It's a fundraiser for Habitat for Humanity. Anyway, the cotillion happens this weekend so maybe she's feeling overwhelmed." He shook his head. "Plus, she's been a little blue this Christmas, which is understandable."

"You mean because of your father's condition?"

"Huh?" His brow creased. "Well, sure, we've always been close. We spend holidays together, along with a few other neighbors. That's always a good time."

Now Carol was confused. Why wouldn't they spend holidays together as a family? Then she thought about her Christmas plans—wasn't she running away from her family just now?

"And, man, the food we cook up for our Christmas Eve party," Victor continued. "We spend most of the day fixing an

Italian feast at our house, then we take it all over to Maria's in the late afternoon." He smacked his lips. "We eat and celebrate all night—and the next day too. And take it from me, it's good eatin' in the neighborhood." He chuckled. "I'm a serious foodie. Especially when it comes to Italian dishes. And I'm a pretty decent chef too, if I do say so. I used to own my own restaurant in the city. I sold it to come home and help my parents, but I hope to open another someday . . . when the time is right." Now he began to list some of the Sicilian dishes he and his mom would be preparing for Christmas Eve.

Carol suddenly felt her stomach rumbling. "Wow, that all sounds delicious."

"Well, trust me, if you're still here at Christmastime, you won't find better food in all of Michigan." He grinned.

"Oh, I'll be in the Bahamas by then." She still felt a little confused about the way he was describing his family. "You say you cook and then take the food over to Maria's. I thought you lived with your parents." She didn't want to sound too nosy. "But maybe your parents don't live in the same house? Or is your dad in some kind of memory care place?"

"No, Dad's still at home. But my mom's worried it might be his last year there. I'll admit he's a handful. Trying to help her with Dad, plus get all the farm chores done, keeps me running."

"Maybe I can help you out while I'm here."

His brows arched as if her offer was surprising. "Thanks, but your time's limited. You should probably focus your attention on Maria."

Wouldn't that be helping him? She felt even more puzzled, but the more questions she asked, the foggier things got.

"So when was the last time you saw Maria?" he asked as he turned down another rural road. This one hadn't been plowed yet so it was extra slow going. She wondered how much farther it would be. She was starting to feel slightly dazed by all the swirling white, and lost, as if they were in the middle of nowhere.

"Never," she replied.

"Really?" He paused at a stop sign and turned toward her. "But you stay in touch?"

"I've never spoken with her before today. Maria and my mother have been estranged since before I was born. I'm not really sure why. But then my mom baffles me in a lot of ways." She shook her head. "She's, uh, kind of a character." That was an understatement!

"So you don't know about Don then?"

"You mean about his Alzheimer's?" she asked. Was he as zoned out as he sounded? Maybe the snow was making him dizzy too. "I know what you've told me just now."

"Huh?" He waved at a pickup plowing a long driveway.

"About your dad?" she reminded him.

"Huh?" he said again. "What do you mean?"

"Didn't you just tell me Uncle Don is sick?"

"I never said that."

"You said your dad has Alzheimer's." She could hear the sharp edge in her voice. "I'll admit I'm tired, but the way you describe your family is really confusing me."

"My dad *does* have Alzheimer's." He sounded defensive. "But your uncle Don was never sick. He was perfectly healthy until the tractor rolled over while he was plowing the south hill last spring."

"What?" She shook her head, trying to make sense of this. "Was that what started his Alzheimer's?"

"No. That's what killed him." Victor actually laughed now. "I'm sorry. It's not funny. It was actually quite tragic. I'm just laughing at how mixed-up this conversation has gotten. Did you think your uncle Don was my dad?"

"Well, isn't Maria your mom?" Now Carol wasn't just confused, she was irritated.

"Of course not. Sure, she's been like a second mom to me, and she and my mom are as close as sisters." He laughed even harder now. "So this whole time, you thought *your* aunt was *my* mom? That would make me your cousin!"

"Hey, give me a break. I haven't slept in a couple days so I'm a space case. Please, forgive me my confusion." She knew her tone was snarky but couldn't help it.

"That's okay. It's probably my fault. Sorry."

"Well, you gotta admit, it was pretty confusing."

"For you maybe." He grinned. "I'm actually relieved we're *not* related."

"I'm sure." She rolled her eyes. "I wouldn't want to be an embarrassment to your family." She pointed at him. "And it was an honest mistake. I mean, we even look a little alike. Wavy hair, dark eyes . . . must be our Italian roots."

His expression softened. "Yeah, I noticed that too." He paused to let another snowplow go by, then made a turn onto a road with deep snowdrifts. He slowly plowed his way through. "This is O'Harneys' property." After a bit of maneuvering, he pulled up to a structure hidden behind a thick curtain of blizzarding snow. "I'll get as close to the porch as I can to let you out."

"Thanks. And thanks for the ride too." She reached for the door handle. "Sorry I was so mixed up about everything."

"No problem. It was pretty entertaining." He opened his door, then hurried to the rear of the truck to dig out her bag from the snow. She trudged through the knee-deep snow and winced at the sharp cold on her bare skin. By the time she got onto the covered porch, he was setting her bag by the front door and pointing to her now snow-covered sandals "I bet your feet are frozen. Anyway, if I don't see you before you leave for the Bahamas, it was nice to meet ya." He tipped his hat and knocked on the door for her. "Tell Maria I had to get moving if I'm going to clear her driveway and our other neighbors' today."

She thanked him as he bounded back down the steps. And suddenly the front door swung open to reveal a white-haired woman with a youthful face. She was wearing faded jeans and a gray sweatshirt. One of her arms was wrapped in a dish towel and was being supported by her other arm. "Come in, come in," she said loud enough to be heard above the howling wind. "Close the door to keep the heat inside."

Carol wheeled her bag in and closed the door. "Whew, that storm is wild."

"I'll say." The woman smiled. "Welcome, Carol. As you probably guessed, I'm your aunt Maria." She nodded toward her wrapped arm. "I'd help with your bag, but I fell early this morning—right before you called. It's probably a sprain, so I'm icing it."

"Oh, dear. I'm sorry."

"It was my own dumb fault. I miscalculated a step on my ladder and took a tumble. Bad move on my part."

"Sounds like my visit is bad timing on my part." Carol grimaced. Hadn't Victor mentioned something like that?

"Not at all." Maria shook her head. "I'm thrilled to meet you." She checked Carol from head to toe now. "You're a very pretty girl too, Carol. You look like a real Banducci."

"Thank you. I never thought I looked much like my mom."

"No, she takes after your grandma. She wasn't Italian. But you definitely resemble the Banducci side of the family."

"Thanks."

"Come on in by the fire." Maria led her into the living room. "Fortunately, I got it started before I fell. It's still warm but on its way out. I didn't much feel like going out for a load of wood."

"I can do that for you," Carol offered. "I'd like to be helpful while I'm here."

"Not in that getup." Maria frowned at Carol's inappropriate footwear. "My goodness, is that what you've been wearing out in this snow?"

"I, uh, I thought I'd be in the Bahamas by now," she admitted dismally.

"Well, you must be freezing. You'll catch pneumonia in those things."

"Unfortunately, I only packed summer clothes and not many of those. My options are limited, but I can still get some wood. Just point me in the direction and—"

"Not until you get some warmer clothes on. Follow me," Maria ordered, leading her through the comfortably furnished room. They approached a closed door. "Open that."

Carol obeyed, then switched on the light to see an attractive master bedroom. "Pretty room," she commented as Maria went to another closed door.

"Thanks. I redid the whole room for our fiftieth anniversary a couple years ago. Open that." She waited as Carol did as asked. "Get one of those sweaters from that shelf, or a sweatshirt, or whatever suits your fancy," she said. "And see those fleece-lined slippers on the floor in the corner? Don got them for me last Christmas, but I hardly ever remember to wear them. I'm not sure if they'll fit you right, but they should work for the time being."

Carol pulled out a warm-looking Nordic sweater with a snowflake design. "Is this okay?"

"Sure. Take whatever you like. Take a flannel shirt too. Then we'll find you some warm socks in the dresser. I've got blue jeans, too, if you want. You actually look about my height. They might be a little baggy on you, but you can belt 'em in if you need to."

Carol, fully loaded down with winter clothes, followed her aunt back to the living room, where Maria pointed to the wood-carved staircase. "There are more bedrooms up there. The first door on your right is already made up for guests, not that I'd planned on anyone anytime soon. I just like to keep it ready.

The room faces south, so on a clear day, it gets lots of sunshine in the wintertime. I'd suggest you get yourself set up in there."

"I'll just be a few minutes," Carol called from halfway up the stairs.

"Perfect. How are you at making coffee? I'm missing my morning java."

"I'm a pro," she called back. "I'll hurry."

"Take your time. That fire'll keep for a bit."

Just the same, Carol hurried. The guest bedroom was charming with its white metal headboard and patchwork quilt in varying shades of sage green and lavender. As she sat in an old oak rocker and tugged the warm clothing over her chilled limbs, she checked out the room more. The celery-green walls were decorated with handsome pastoral prints of sheep, pastures, and peaceful landscapes. The braided rug gave warmth to the golden hardwood floors, and the antique oak armoire, topped with a large, white pitcher of dried lavender, added even more personality. Old-fashioned perhaps, but this motif worked nicely with the old farmhouse. It didn't feel overdone or flashy like Carol's mother liked to decorate. Aunt Maria had good taste.

Carol glanced at her image in the mirror above the dresser. Maria's clothes were a bit loose but not bad. She nosed around the other upstairs rooms, hoping there would be a bathroom, and was rewarded with a big bathroom that was just as handsome as the guest bedroom. The sage-and-lavender theme continued. Only instead of green, its walls were a very pale shade of lavender. The white claw-foot tub and cushy towels were very inviting! Even if she was only here overnight, it would be an enjoyable visit.

She rushed back downstairs and found her aunt in the kitchen, struggling to fill a coffee carafe. Carol intervened. "Let me get that going for you."

"Thanks." Maria stepped back. "There are coffee beans in

that glass jar there and filters in the top drawer. Do you know how to use a grinder?"

"You bet. I always grind my own beans too."

"Don used to say the only good coffee must be made within five minutes of grinding."

"Smart man."

"Looks like those clothes are working for you," Maria observed from where she'd seated herself at the kitchen table.

"You were right. We are nearly the same size." Carol paused as she ran the grinder. "By the way, I have to compliment you on your decor upstairs—and all throughout your house, for that matter. I really like your taste." As she filled the filter and got the coffee brewing, she told Maria about her job in interior design. "I've mostly been doing staging though. Not exactly the career I'd hoped for, but I guess I'm paying my dues." She told her a bit about all the holiday decorating she'd been doing the past couple of months. "That's one reason I wanted to go to the Bahamas," she confessed. "To escape all the 'deck the halls fa la la.' I guess I'm not a real fan of Christmas. Never have been."

"But you're a Christmas baby." Maria's brow creased. "Though maybe that makes some sense then. Anyway, that's very interesting that you got a degree in interior design." Her tone sounded a bit dreamy. "I always loved interior decorating too. If I'd gone on to get a degree, I might've pursued something like that. Don used to make fun of me. He'd say that he couldn't be gone from the house for more than a day out of fear that I'd have our house rearranged and redone before he got back." She chuckled. "But at least I'm a DIY gal. I never pay anyone for something I can do myself."

"Well, you've done a good job," Carol said as she wiped some stray coffee grounds from the obviously upgraded marble countertop. "Now point me to the firewood."

"First I'll point you to my snow boots." Maria stood slowly, wincing in pain.

"Are you okay?"

"Well, it definitely hurts. I have an elastic wrap I might let you help me with after you get the wood in."

"Hopefully I can still remember the first aid class I took in college."

Maria led the way to a back porch and pointed to several pairs of boots lined up by a worn wooden bench. "Take your pick."

"These look warm." Carol picked up fleece-lined boots and then sat on the bench to put them on. "Since your slippers fit perfectly, I'm guessing these will too."

"And get yourself a parka," Maria nodded to a row of coats hanging on hooks. "That green one with the hood is the warmest. Just make sure to zip it up before you go out." She sighed. "I'm sure glad you can help me, Carol. I've always been so independent. Notorious for not allowing anyone to help me. Even Don." She looked down at her arm glumly. "Maybe the good Lord is teaching me a lesson, forcing me into an uncomfortable situation and making me needy."

Carol wanted to echo "me too." It felt possible that the good Lord was trying to teach her a lesson about neediness too. It was hard to admit it, even to herself, but this longing deep within her felt like a cry for family.

C arol didn't have time to check the airlines until she got the firewood inside, had served and cleaned up a late breakfast, and wrapped her aunt's arm securely. But flights were still canceled and, according to the weather channels, the whole country was snarled up with the "most widespread winter storm the country has seen in decades." Whatever that meant.

"How's your arm feeling now?" Carol asked as she encouraged her aunt to rest with her ice pack. She was worried her aunt wasn't taking her injury seriously enough. "You still don't think it needs an X-ray? I'm no expert, but I do think it could be broken. I could drive us—"

"Thanks. But we don't need to go driving around in this blizzard," Maria said firmly—and not for the first time. "Whatever is wrong with my arm will still be going on when the storm lets up. I'm in no danger."

"I suppose driving would put us both in danger . . ." Carol thought of the cars strewn along the highway earlier that morning. "Especially since I'm not comfortable in these driving conditions." She looked at her aunt, who was holding her arm very gingerly. "How about some more ibuprofen? It's been almost four hours. And maybe some fresh ice?"

Maria conceded to both, and Carol scurried around playing nurse. She didn't mind helping her aunt. In fact, it was kind of nice to be needed like this. Part of her was even relieved that flights weren't going out yet. And she wondered what it would be like to spend Christmas here.

After Maria had fresh ice and ibuprofen as well as a mug of spice tea, Carol asked more about the fall that morning.

"Silly me." Maria shook her head. "I was feeling guilty for not having any Christmas decorations up yet, especially since the Clarksons—that's Victor's family—are coming here on Christmas Eve. As well as some neighbors. I'm known for having the place decked to the nines, but I'm on slow speed this year." She paused to sip her tea. "So, anyway, I forced myself to go up to the attic this morning. That's where I keep all my Christmas decor. It's all boxed and sorted and actually makes the process of decorating fairly simple. Well, usually. I started with the top shelf, which requires my stepladder. I had a box of garlands and lights in my hands. Not heavy, mind you. I like to swag them around banisters and doorways and over the porch railing. It's very pretty in the snow. Well, not in a blizzard. But it would be after it all stops and the world out there is blanketed in white." She glanced out the window, then pursed her lips. "It will quit . . . eventually."

Carol blew the top of the tea in her mug. It was some kind of cinnamon blend and warmed her nicely.

"Anyway, getting the swags up seemed like a festive way to start my decorating. I planned to come down and put some holiday music on and get into the spirit. So go the plans of mice and men." She wrinkled her nose. "I had the box balanced in one hand and was going down the ladder in a way I thought was safe, but I miscounted my steps and—kaboom—down I went. I tried to catch myself, and I suppose my arm got mangled up beneath me somehow."

"Sounds traumatic."

Maria gave a wry smile. "All I know is I was the only thing that got decorated. I probably looked like a Christmas tree with strands of faux greens and lights all over me. I somehow got untangled. My arm was throbbing by the time I made it down, and I felt so miserable and considered just giving up. That's about when you called." She looked at Carol with misty eyes. "You really feel like a godsend. Even if this is just a brief visit, I'm so glad you're here. I've always wanted to meet you. I used to invite your mother to bring you up here year after year, but she always had an excuse." She cleared her throat. "Probably my fault."

Carol wanted to ask her to expound on their rift a bit more. Especially since her mother had always been very tight-lipped about her older sister. But the phone rang. Startled by the sound of a landline, Carol leaped to her feet. "Want me to get it?"

"Yes." Maria nodded. "Thank you."

Following the sound of the loud ringing, she discovered the phone on a little table in the hallway. Carol answered.

"Hey, is this Carol?" Victor asked brightly. "I figured you must still be there since I heard no flights are going out today. Is Maria busy?"

"Well, no. But she's kind of resting." She quietly explained about her aunt's arm. "I'm worried it could be broken, but she doesn't want to get it checked. Not in this weather, anyway."

"That's too bad. I'm not surprised she wants to wait for the roads to clear. It's pretty gnarly out there. The reason I called is to see if I can bring her a Christmas tree. I picked up a couple of beauties from Harper's Tree Farm this afternoon. Got 'em for free after I plowed their drive. I hoped to drop one by, but if Maria's laid up . . . maybe not. What do you think?"

Carol wasn't sure what she thought. Wasn't it holiday decorations that sidelined her aunt today? "Well, I could ask her."

"Thanks," Victor said. "And tell her I'll get the tree in the house and set it up for her. I can even help decorate it if she wants."

Carol had zero interest in anything to do with Christmas, but she thought she might enjoy seeing Victor again, and so when she told her aunt about the tree, she made it sound cheerful and positive. "He said he'd get it all set up for you too," she said finally.

"Well, if he really has time," Maria said, uncertain. "I guess it'd be okay."

"He even offered to decorate it for you," Carol added. "But I can help out."

Maria's brows arched. "I thought you were sick of all that Christmas fa la la and that you just wanted to escape it all, to run away to the Bahamas. Sure you want to get involved in decorating?" There almost seemed to be a teasing tone to her question.

Carol felt her cheeks warm as she considered her answer. Was this sudden change of heart because she wanted to help her aunt? Or was it due to the guy waiting on the phone? "Well, this feels different," she said. "It's for family." She smiled. That was true. "And for your neighbors since I know you like to host them here." That was true too.

Maria just nodded and smiled in a slightly smug way.

As Carol headed back to the phone with Maria's answer, she could hear a muffled chuckle behind her. Apparently, Maria was amused by all this. Oh well.

"I can't get it over there until later today," Victor told her. "Still got plowing to finish while there's daylight. Is that okay?"

"Okay by me. I'm not going anywhere. Well, not until flights resume, at least. And from what I've heard, that's not likely. Not until tomorrow anyway."

"Right."

As she ended the call, she decided to recheck the airline's site to see if they'd made any progress yet. To her surprise, they were rebooking twenty-four hours out now. The available Miami flights weren't until tomorrow afternoon, but she went ahead and nabbed one for 5:40 anyway. Pacing in front of the woodstove, which she noted could use more wood, she waited for the confirmation. Then, satisfied that she would be on her way by the next day, she pocketed her phone.

However, as she pulled on the green parka and tugged on the fleece-lined boots, she wondered why she felt so torn about leaving. What was wrong with her? Did she really want to remain here as Aunt Maria's houseguest? Even for a few days? No, that was ridiculous! Besides her careless packing, she hadn't even gotten travel insurance for this whole Bahamian vacation. If she canceled everything now, she would lose money—and miss out on those sunny beaches. No, she was definitely leaving. Still, she decided not to mention it to Maria just yet. Why worry her?

* * * *

After a light lunch fixed by Carol, Maria spent the afternoon napping in her recliner while Carol sat on the soft chenille sofa near the woodstove and stoked the crackling fire. She felt surprisingly refreshed. Outside, snow was still falling and though it was half past five, darkness had fully set in. But inside, all felt cozy and secure and warm. A little while later, Maria woke and stretched.

"Can you turn on the porch light for Victor?" Maria asked. "I'm thinking he'll be here before long. And would you pull the drapes while you're up?"

"Of course." Carol saw to the tasks and brought in some more pieces of wood too. She carefully stacked them in the antique copper washtub Maria used for firewood. As she unzipped her parka, she studied Maria, wondering why her brow was creased. "Are you in pain?" she asked.

Maria shifted slightly. "Yes, a little."

"No wonder. You haven't had ibuprofen in hours. Let me get you some."

She hurried to the kitchen, then shook two pills from the

bottle and filled a glass with water. Poor Maria. She'd probably been in pain for a while now. But in the short time Carol had observed her aunt, she pegged her as the type who would suffer in silence. And Carol should know about that. Wasn't that the way she was wired too? Not for the first time, Carol was struck by the similarities in her and her aunt. Carol was more like her than her own mother.

She took the pills to Maria, then waited for her to take them.

"Now"—Carol took the empty glass back—"what can I fix you for dinner?"

Maria's brow furrowed. "Well, that's a good question. I didn't take anything out of the freezer, and I'm afraid my fridge is a little bare. I'd meant to get to the grocery store today. Although my freezer is well-stocked with beef and—" She was interrupted by the sound of the doorbell. "That must be Victor. Let him in and we'll figure out dinner later. How do you feel about tuna?"

Carol laughed as she headed for the door. "It's a standby at my house." She opened the door to a gust of wind and a good-looking guy well-dusted with snow.

"Ho, ho, ho," he said heartily. "Anyone need a Christmas tree here?"

"Come in, come in," Carol said. "Before all the cold air comes with you." Then she went outside to help him get the tree into the house. She was glad to see he'd already secured a stand to its trunk. But the bushy tree took a bit of finagling to get it all the way inside. When they finally closed the front door, Victor sat the tree upright, albeit a little cockeyed in the tree stand.

"It's a handsome tree." Carol inhaled deeply. "And it smells amazing."

"They called it a concolor fir. Don't think that's its scientific name, but I guess it's supposed to smell like oranges."

"It does." She nodded with enthusiasm. "Very citrusy."

"Well, bring that tree in here," Maria called from her recliner. "Let's see it."

Victor managed the tree on his own and set it in the center of the living room. "What do you think?"

"It's crooked." Now Maria beamed at him. "But absolutely beautiful. Thank you so much, Victor."

"Do you want it right there like usual?" He pointed to the front window, where Carol had just closed the drapes.

"Yes, but we'll have to move a few things." Maria shifted in the chair, looking as if she was about to get up.

"You stay put," Victor commanded. "Carol and I got this."

Maria leaned back with pursed lips. "Fine. I'll be a silent spectator then."

"No need to be silent. You can be the director," Carol said as she reached for one of the plants from the marble tabletop flanking the window. "Where should we relocate these plants?"

"Put them on that lowboy dresser in my bedroom," Maria told her. "The light's not quite as good, but they'll be okay for a couple of weeks. But could you put a towel beneath them to protect the dresser top? It was Don's mother's."

"Consider it done," Carol told her.

"The linen closet is down that hall," Maria called.

Before long, Carol had a heavy towel in place and was setting up the first two plants. Then Victor came in with a couple more. Carol moved a framed wedding photo to make more room, then paused to really study it. "Is this Maria and Don?" she asked incredulously.

"Looks like it to me." He leaned closer to peer at it. "She was a real beauty with that long thick dark hair and dark eyes." He looked from the photo to Carol, then blinked. "Man, you two could be twins."

"There's definitely a family resemblance." She set the photo back down, eyes still fixed on the happy couple. "Judging by the clothes and hair, I'm guessing they were married in the 1970s."

"Sounds like a good guess to me." He nodded, still staring at Carol with a hard-to-read expression.

"I'll help you move that table." Feeling uncomfortable with his focused attention, she moved toward the door. "It might be small, but it looks heavy."

Maria instructed them to put the table near the front door. "I always set the nativity on it for my guests to see as they enter the house."

"Yeah, I remember being fascinated by that when I was little," Victor said as they transported the table. "The pieces looked so real."

With a few other moves and tweaks, they got the tree into place and, after a little more finessing, got it standing up straighter in the stand. "I'll get some water for it," Carol offered.

"Oh, I almost forgot," Victor said suddenly. "Mom sent over some dinner."

Maria sounded surprised. "Dinner?"

"If you already ate, you can have it tomorrow. It's just a lasagna that she took out of the freezer to make room for some Christmas cookies. I think she was trying to hide them from Dad. His sweet tooth is out of control." He grinned. "But I have to admit I snuck a few too."

"Antonia's lasagna!" Maria's eyes lit up. "How kind of her. I'm glad to say we haven't eaten dinner yet."

"And"—his tone lilted at the end of the word—"if you ladies don't mind my company, well, I brought some salad fixings that I could throw together for you."

"Of course, you're invited." Maria nodded eagerly. "Victor is a fine chef," she told Carol. "His salads are beyond just salad."

"It all sounds good to me," Carol said. "I'm not much good in the kitchen, but I do know how to set a nice table."

"Well, you kids go make yourself at home in my kitchen and I will just sit here and be spoiled," Maria said happily.

Victor laughed. "That'll be quite a change for you. Might as well enjoy it."

"Yes," Carol agreed, but almost added "while you can" since she knew her aunt would be on her own by tomorrow evening. Well, unless this storm refused to let up . . . and she was almost hoping that it wouldn't.

5

While Victor was creating a gorgeous green salad with colorful peppers and gorgonzola and a few other interesting ingredients, Carol set the dining room table. Finished but not satisfied that it was festive enough, Carol asked Maria if she could bring a few things down from the attic.

"You know, to decorate the tree." She pushed up the sleeves of the heavy sweater Maria had lent her. For the first time today, she was almost too warm.

"Maybe you should change into something a bit more comfortable first," Maria suggested. "Unless you're planning to go out for some cross-country skiing tonight."

Carol laughed. "No thanks, but that's a good idea." On her way to the attic, she stopped by the guest room and changed into a plaid flannel shirt she'd borrowed. Tucking it into her pants, she took a moment to bundle her thick hair into a ponytail, then trekked up to the attic, which—other than a spilled box of greens and lights—was impressively organized. Not sure what to bring down, she boxed up the garlands and spilled decor. Then, after taking everything to the living room, she returned to randomly select a couple more boxes and brought them down too.

Spotting some interesting items, she decided to give the dining room table a holiday flair. She knew Maria would like it. She was just lighting some candles amid some sparkly ornaments and faux greens when Victor appeared with two glasses of red wine. "One for Maria and for you, if you like."

She reached for the goblet. "I like."

"Great!" He handed it to her, then called into the living room. "Soup's on, Maria." Then he headed into the living room to help her from the chair. Once she was on her feet, he held out the wine like a carrot before a donkey. "The feast awaits, your highness."

Maria just laughed, but the sparkle in her eyes suggested she was enjoying the attention. But her face really lit up when she came into the dining room. "Oh, my goodness!" she exclaimed. "This is beautiful! Carol, did you put this together?"

Carol shrugged. "They're your ornaments and candles and things."

"Well, I've never arranged them like this. It's so pretty."

"And dinner is coming," he said as he helped her to the head of the table.

"I really do feel like royalty," she said, sitting down.

"Good." Carol took the chair adjacent to her. "After your rough morning, you deserve a break." She wrinkled her nose. "Just not a broken arm."

Victor returned with the steaming lasagna and colorful salad, then went back to the kitchen for a couple more things. When they were all finally seated, he lifted his glass in a toast. "Here's to Maria getting better soon." Then he turned to Carol with a more serious expression. "And here's to Carol getting to her final destination in time for Christmas."

They all clinked glasses and then Maria bowed her head to ask a blessing and to express gratitude for her young friends helping her in a time of need. She echoed Victor's toast by praying that God get Carol safely to "where she needs to be for Christmas." Interestingly, neither of them had mentioned the Bahamas . . . and more and more Carol wondered.

"For someone who despises Christmas as much as you do, you're certainly being a good sport, Carol," Maria said as Victor served the lasagna.

Victor actually dropped the serving spatula. "What? Carol hates Christmas?"

"Well, hate is a strong word." Carol set her wineglass down with a thunk.

"I'm sorry, Carol." Maria looked contrite. "I probably spoke out of turn."

Carol shrugged self-consciously. "Well, it's not something I usually advertise. In fact, I don't think I've ever told anyone before."

"Not even your parents?" Maria asked.

"No, they wouldn't understand."

"But why?" Victor returned to serving lasagna. "How could anyone hate Christmas? I mean, I get that the holiday gets a little extreme with materialism and pressure and all that. But it's Christmas."

Carol wasn't even sure how to answer.

"I'm sorry. I really shouldn't have said anything," Maria repeated. "You see, Christmas is Carol's birthday, and I think it wasn't a particularly happy day for her growing up." She paused to fork her salad. "Her parents' marriage was, well, a little rocky. And besides that, this poor woman has been decorating houses for Christmas since Halloween."

Carol was surprised how well Maria could explain her feelings toward the holiday. Apparently she'd been listening better than Carol realized and was actually sympathetic.

"Well, I guess that makes sense." Victor still appeared concerned. "And considering all that, you really are being a good sport, Carol. Stuck in Michigan with weather like this. It must be a real letdown compared to the Bahamas."

She suppressed the urge to confess she had already rebooked her flight. She didn't want to spoil this lovely meal. "It's not such a letdown. I'm actually enjoying this unexpected visit with Aunt Maria," she told him. "It was way overdue."

"I agree. It was overdue." Maria lifted her wineglass. "Here's to enjoying what time we have while we have it, right?"

"Vivere il momento!" Victor exclaimed.

"Yes!" Maria nodded. "Live in the moment."

"Salute!" Carol chimed in with one of the few Italian words she could remember, and they echoed her toast. As they ate, she realized she hadn't had a meal this delicious in ages. Maybe never. Despite her mom's Italian heritage, she had never cooked anything like this. And Carol had never really learned the art of cooking herself. As a single woman, she usually stocked her freezer with microwaveable meals or got by on salad from a bag with a bit of protein on top. Nothing to brag about.

"This was so good," she said after clearing her plate.

Victor reached for the lasagna pan. "More?"

"No thanks. I'm stuffed." She sighed with contentment. "And I'm not exaggerating when I say this might be the best meal I've ever eaten."

"Really?" He looked surprised. "It's just lasagna and salad."

"The lasagna was fabulous . . . and the salad was amazing."

"Well, thanks." He grinned.

"Thank you," she told him.

"Thank you both," Maria said. "I wish I could offer you dessert."

"If you don't mind my imposition, I noticed you have some chocolate gelato in the freezer." Victor was already gathering plates. "And I could make some espresso." He paused by Maria. "If you still have your espresso maker."

"I do. I keep it in that appliance cabinet," she told him, pointing.

"Right. I'll go throw something together."

"Let me help." Carol picked up the lasagna dish and salad bowl and followed him back to the kitchen. Then, as he made espresso and dished out gelato, complete with some little short-bread cookies he found in a cupboard, she rinsed the dishes and loaded them into the dishwasher. She closed the appliance door just as Victor finished arranging an attractive dessert tray.

With arms crossed in front of her, she looked on as he set dainty spoons next to the Christmassy cocktail napkins he'd found in a drawer. "That looks very professional."

"Too much?" His smile looked a little cheesy. "After all my years in the restaurant business, it's hard to do anything half-way."

She smiled. "I think it's very nice."

He picked up the tray, then paused to look at her. "Well, I thought since it's your last—and only night here—why not make it special."

She felt her brows arch. "How did you know I rebooked a flight for tomorrow?"

"I just figured." His eyes darkened. "I'm sure Maria is dis-appointed."

"I haven't told her yet. I wanted to make this evening a happy one."

He brightened. "Good for you."

She held the swinging door open for him as they returned to the dining room. Maria beamed at both of them. "How lovely!"

The visit remained fun and friendly as they enjoyed dessert and espresso. When they were all finished, Carol insisted on cleaning up. "I might not be much of a cook, but I'm good on cleanup."

"Okay," Victor agreed. "I'll escort Queen Maria back to her throne, then I can start bringing down some Christmas orna-ments and things for the tree."

As Carol took the tray of dishes to the kitchen, she heard Maria chatting merrily with Victor. And even though Carol felt a little deceitful for keeping tomorrow's travel plans to herself, it was worth it to hear the happiness in her aunt's voice.

Besides, she rationalized as she put the last of the things in the dishwasher and turned it on, who knew what tomorrow would bring? Perhaps the weather would trap her here longer—and really, would that be such a bad thing?

As she left the kitchen, she overheard Maria and Victor talking.

"So, are you still dating Victoria?" Maria asked.

"I guess you could say that." Victor's answer sounded a little evasive, but maybe he didn't like Maria prying into his personal life. Carol paused in the dining room, still listening.

"You two have been dating for quite some time," Maria persisted. "Any plans to make it permanent? Any diamond rings showing up for Christmas?"

"Oh, Maria." Victor sounded a little exasperated. "You still hoping to marry me off?"

"You could do worse than Victoria." Maria's tone sounded slightly sarcastic.

"Really? I thought you never cared for her."

"I said you could do worse," Maria teased. "Not that you couldn't do better."

Victor just laughed, then inquired about a box of ornaments he'd seen upstairs, clearly changing the subject. "They're interesting but look pretty old. Do you want me to bring them down?"

"Oh, I don't think so. They were Don's mother's. We put them up while she was alive, but they never really fit in with the ones I like to use. Still, they're probably vintage so I hate to get rid of them."

Feeling guilty for eavesdropping, Carol cleared her throat as she entered the room. "Should I bring down anything else from the attic?" she asked. She took in the stacks of cardboard boxes and plastic bins strewn across the living room floor and shook her head. "Never mind. That looks like plenty."

"They're not all for the tree," Maria explained. "But I asked him to bring down everything on the storage shelf up there. They're the ones I use every year. Thought that would save us time later." She winked at Carol. "After seeing your creativity with my dining room table, I've decided to put you in charge of all the decor. That is, if you don't mind." Maria's smile dimmed. "Except I forgot about your aversion to Christmas. I'm sorry."

"No, no, that's okay," Carol assured her. "This is different. This is for family, not work. It'll be fun." Still, she wondered how much she'd be able to finish before it was time for her to leave tomorrow. For that matter, she wasn't even sure how she'd get to the airport. Victor had seemed unenthused about her travel plans, so he might not be willing to take her. Perhaps she could get an Uber. It would be expensive, but after her free lodging and meal, the fee was nothing.

"To be honest, I've never done this before. Not without my mom's supervision." Victor removed a lid from a box marked "tree ornaments." Lifting a star-shaped wooden ornament, he looked puzzled. "Where do we begin?"

"Lights," she proclaimed. "You might need a stepladder for that."

As he went to the back porch for a stepladder, she began opening boxes and putting together a plan. "These ornaments are really sweet, Maria. It looks like you have kind of a farm and animal theme going."

"Yes. I started collecting them in the early years of our marriage, when having our own farm was still a dream. I added to them over the years."

Carol dangled a sweet little porcelain lamb on its wire hanger. "This is darling."

A shadow darkened Maria's expression. "Oh, yes, that . . . I didn't know it was in there."

"Does it have significance?"

"It was for our first baby."

"Oh . . . I didn't realize you had children." Carol handed the lamb to Maria.

"Well, we tried," she said glumly. "It took years for me to get pregnant. Finally I did. It was autumn of 1984. Don was so excited, he got me this little lamb to commemorate our baby's birth. I was due the following summer." She sighed.

Carol suspected this story had an unhappy ending.

"I miscarried that spring . . . and was never able to get pregnant again."

"I'm sorry." Carol didn't know what else to say.

"I was so happy for your mother when she had you that following Christmas." Maria's smile looked forced. "I sent her a gift for you but never heard back. I continued to try reaching out, but Rosa wanted nothing to do with me."

"I know you always sent us Christmas cards," Carol said weakly, afraid to mention that her mother always tossed them in the trash. Sometimes unopened.

"Birthday cards, too, although I wasn't sure if they reached you or not."

Carol didn't know what to say. "Well, no matter now." Maria looked down at the little lamb. "It really is a cute ornament. I think I'd like it to go on the tree this year."

Victor returned with the ladder and, with Carol's direction, proceeded to string up the lights, followed by garlands of red wooden beads that looked like ripe cranberries. As she helped him with the lower strands, Carol mulled over what Maria had just told her. Her aunt's pregnancy coincided with the year Carol had been born. She wondered if her unborn cousin had been a boy or a girl but knew she couldn't ask. Instead, she focused on decorating the tree. With Victor's help—and his ability to follow her direction—it didn't take as long as she expected. Soon the emptied boxes were stacked by the stairs, and the big moment came.

"Look," Carol said quietly to Victor, pointing toward Maria

who was soundly asleep, the little white lamb still in her good hand.

"Should I plug it in yet?" Victor asked.

"Maybe we should wake her first," Carol said. "I hate to, but she'd need to go to bed, anyway."

Victor nodded, then gently nudged Maria. "Hey, beautiful, time to wake up. We're about to light the tree."

Maria slowly blinked and came to life as Victor returned to the outlet. "Ready?"

Then just as Maria turned toward the tree, Victor plugged it in. "Ta-da!"

"Oh, my!" Her eyes were as wide as a child's on Christmas morning. "That is beautiful. The best it's ever looked."

Carol was impressed too. "I was worried we put too many things on, but it does look festive."

Now Maria broke into "O, Christmas Tree," and Victor and Carol did their best to sing along with her, humming when they couldn't remember all the words. They broke into laughter partway through.

"Never mind," Maria said. "Thank you both. It's lovely."

"I hate to be a party pooper, but I am seriously tired." Carol let out a sleepy yawn. "Despite my afternoon nap and the time difference, I don't think I recovered from spending last night at the airport."

"I don't have those excuses, but I'm tired too," Victor admitted. "Again, thank you, ladies, for allowing me to join you this evening."

"Thank you for the tree and the dinner!" Maria began to ease herself up from the recliner, and Victor stepped forward to help her. Then Carol escorted Maria to her bedroom as he got his coat and things and exited out the front door.

"Do you need help getting ready for bed?" Carol asked her aunt.

"Oh, I don't think so."

"But your arm? Won't undressing and everything be diffi-cult?" She pointed to Maria's plaid shirt. "Especially with those buttons?"

Maria smiled sheepishly. "Yes, I suppose that could be pain-ful."

"Plus you need some more ibuprofen," Carol reminded her.

It took a bit of time, and some careful manipulating, but Maria was finally in her nightgown and ready for bed. "I sup-pose I did need help," she confessed after Carol pointed out the pills and a glass of water on her bedside table.

"If you need me, you can just call out." Carol wasn't sure she'd be able to hear all the way upstairs. "Or maybe you have a bell? You could ring for me?"

"No, that's silly. I'll be fine." Maria eased herself to the edge of her bed. "You get to sleep, Carol. You must be exhausted." She smiled wearily. "I hope that bed is comfortable. I replaced the mattress last year, and my sister-in-law claimed it was too soft." She rolled her eyes. "But then again, Cynthia complains about most everything."

"Well, I like a soft mattress." Carol peeled the quilt back even farther so Maria could climb into bed. "I'm sure it'll be just fine. Good night, Aunt Maria."

Maria's face lit up. "Sweet dreams, dear."

As Carol went up the stairs, she felt bittersweet. She already loved her aunt—loved being in her home and in her world—and that roused some fresh new hostility toward her own mom for how coldhearted she'd been to ignore her older sister their entire adult life. Carol had no idea what had originally caused the estrangement, but as a child, she'd sided with her mom, assuming she had an "evil older sister" who'd done something horrible to make her so bitter. Now Carol realized there were two sides to this story, and she suspected her sympathies would lie with her aunt. But that didn't feel very good . . . especially since Carol had been trying to forgive her mother.

6

The soft bed in Maria's guest room was far more comfortable than Carol's mattress at home, so Carol awoke refreshed and rested the next morning. But she was shocked to discover it was already almost nine. She never slept that late! But remembering it was only six in Seattle made her feel a little better. Still, worried that Maria could be awake and needing help, she quickly pulled on jeans and a sweater, then slid her feet into the warm slippers she'd left by the bed and hurried downstairs. She found Maria wearing a purple bathrobe like a shawl and standing by the opened woodstove with a piece of firewood in her good hand.

"Hey, let me take care of that." Carol removed the log from her hand. "Sorry for oversleeping."

"I'm sure you were exhausted after your travels."

"And I forgot about the time difference."

"No worries. I only got up a few minutes ago. That's late for me." Maria glanced at the woodstove, then back to Carol. "I suppose we don't really need a fire. I do have a furnace with central heating. I just like the feel of wood heat. It seems warmer somehow. Or maybe it's seeing the flames through the glass door."

"It does make things cozier." Carol wadded up some

newspaper. "But I might need some coaching on how to get this started. I was never in Girl Scouts and haven't had a fireplace before." With Maria's instructions, Carol soon had a fire going. She stood, brushing off her hands. "How about some coffee?"

"A girl after my own heart." Maria turned to gaze at the Christmas tree. "Do you think you could plug that in first?"

"Of course." She stooped by the outlet and, plugging in the lights, nodded with satisfaction. She and Victor really had done a first-rate job last night.

"It makes it so cheerful in here." Maria headed for her chair.

"I agree. Let me help you with your robe."

Maria groaned as they maneuvered the robe around her bandaged arm. "I hate being so useless."

"It's a temporary condition," Carol reminded her.

"I suppose, but it sure is bad timing with the holidays and the weather and all."

"How's the pain today? Any improvement?" Carol studied her aunt's face as she eased herself into the chair.

"I'll admit it was throbbing when I first got up, but I took the ibuprofen you set out for me and it is definitely helping now."

"I really think you need an X-ray."

"We'll see about that." Maria, still clutching her sore arm, seemed to shiver. Was it from the chill or was she apprehensive about medical help? As Carol nabbed a colorful afghan from the sofa, she wondered about her aunt's health insurance. Perhaps she couldn't afford a doctor's visit. She gently laid the blanket over her and tucked it around Maria's legs. "How's that until the fire gets going?"

"Perfect. Thank you. Victor's mama, Antonia, gave me this afghan as a thank-you for helping with Larry. It's a granny square pattern. She found it at a craft fair." She ran a hand over the blanket. "Larry thought it was too loud, but I just love it."

"It's very cheerful."

Maria frowned. "I'm afraid I won't be much help to Antonia

and Larry now. Not for a while, anyway. I'm sure glad they've got Victor there. Larry's getting to be a handful for sure, and poor Antonia gets worn out."

"Victor told me about his dad's Alzheimer's. It must be hard on everyone."

Maria tsked and leaned back. "I don't know what they'd do without Victor."

"He seems like a very nice man."

"He is. Not many like him these days. He certainly would be a good catch . . . for the right woman." Maria had a definite twinkle in her eyes now.

Carol just nodded, then turned away. "I'll get the coffee going." She hurried toward the kitchen, suspecting her aunt was hinting at her. But seriously? Did Maria really think she could wave a magic wand and suddenly Victor and Carol would be blissfully strolling down the wedding aisle and living happily ever after? That might work in fairy tales. But not in real life. Not in Carol's real life, anyway.

While the coffee was brewing, Carol perused the fridge for potential breakfast options. Seeing a carton with one lonely brown egg, a partly full milk jug, and not much else, she decided to check the cabinets for other possibilities. Finally deciding that oatmeal might be comforting on a cold winter morning like this, she consulted Maria first.

"Oatmeal sounds lovely. You'll find some homemade applesauce in the pantry. I always like a little in my oatmeal. And there's a jar of walnuts on the counter. I like a few of those too. And a bit of brown sugar, if you don't mind."

"That sounds yummy." Carol smiled. "The coffee's probably almost done. Want me to bring your cup in here?"

"Yes. Bring yours too. There's no hurry on breakfast. It usually takes a while before I'm really hungry."

"Me too," Carol said with enthusiasm.

Returning with their coffees, both black, Carol paused to

admire the glowing Christmas tree. "I can't remember seeing such a pretty tree," she said. "It's not over-the-top, like some of the ones I've done for clients, but just right. And it smells so delicious." She pointed to the still-closed drapes. "Want those opened?"

"Yes, I was just thinking the same thing. Not that anyone will pass by to see our pretty tree, but it will let more light in. Even with the clouds out, the snow is reflective. I don't like being shut up here in the darkness. Don liked the drapes closed. I always told him he'd be a caveman if I allowed it. He claimed he was outside in the sun so much for work, he liked a darkened house. But I always wanted it open and bright. It's one of the few things we disagreed on." She sighed. "But I'd put up with blackout curtains if I could have him back."

"You really miss him, don't you?"

"Every. Single. Day."

Once all the drapes were open, revealing a snowy wonderland, Carol sat on the sofa. "I'm sorry for your loss, Aunt Maria, but I think you were blessed to have such a long, happy marriage. I haven't seen too many of those." To be honest, she couldn't think of one.

"Yes, we were very happy. I'm grateful for all the years we had."

"Still, I'm sure it's been lonely without him."

"I'd be lying if I claimed it wasn't." She peered at Carol over her mug. "You're almost forty, right?"

Carol nodded.

"I'm surprised you're not married by now. Have you been married?"

"No." Carol suppressed aggravation. Why did older women so often think they had the right to ask this question? "I was engaged once."

Maria's brows lifted. "What happened?"

"I realized I didn't love him enough to give everything up for him."

"Give everything up?" Maria looked confused. "Men don't expect women to give up their careers nowadays, do they?"

"No, that's not it." She grimaced at the memory. "Morris was glad I had a steady job. He was an investment broker, and he thought together we could afford a nice house."

"Uh-huh . . . so what went wrong?"

"I wasn't ready to give up being single. I liked having my own place. Making my own choices. To be honest, I don't think I really loved him. Not enough, anyway. And I haven't been in a serious relationship since then. I've dated some men, but always ones who aren't pushing for marriage. I like playing it safe."

Maria appeared dismal. "You young people. So many folks in your generation are afraid of commitment and marriage. I don't understand it. Sure, any relationship has its ups and downs. But having someone beside you, someone you can go through struggles with, spending life with your best friend . . . well, I think it's worth giving up a little independence."

"Maybe so, but maybe it's not for everyone."

"Apparently not for ones like you . . . or Victor either, for that matter. I don't know if that boy will ever get married."

"I overheard you talking to him about a girlfriend . . . Victoria? Maybe there's something going on there with him. You know, you can't force these things." Carol sipped her coffee, trying to appear less interested than she felt.

"Victoria Snyder?" Maria laughed. "I think he only takes her out because it's convenient. Like an excuse for not seeing other girls. But I don't think it's more than that. Not for him, anyway. Although she's a pretty girl, and I've heard she's looking to remarry. But it troubles me that she's already been divorced. You probably know what they say about that."

"What's that?" Carol was glad she hadn't mentioned Morris's failed marriage.

"Divorce rates increase with each marriage. I think of Victor as a son . . . I would never say anything to him, but I don't want him getting hooked by Victoria. Antonia doesn't either."

"What if they're in love? What if it worked out?"

Maria waved a hand. "I can't speak for Victoria, but I don't think she's in love. Not really. And Victor sure doesn't seem to be. We've all seen him get his heart broken once before."

"Really?" Carol couldn't conceal her interest.

Her aunt nodded like she was privy to all the inside stories of Victor's family. And perhaps she was. "His high school sweetheart, Josie Staples. She was a real pretty girl and nice too . . . We all thought they'd tie the knot after college, but in her second year, she met another guy. He was from a wealthy, political family, and soon it was arrivederci, Victor."

"That's too bad."

"Took him years to get over it. He's been pretty cool about marriage ever since. He invested all his time and energy into his restaurant for a while. Antonia thinks it was his therapy. Vittorio's was quite a place. Real popular. Great reviews. Tables by reservation only. And he gave it all up to help his parents. Although, to be fair, COVID hurt the restaurant's business, so maybe it was good timing for a break. I know he hopes to have another restaurant someday. Hopefully right here in Miller's Creek. I'd be his most loyal patron."

"Speaking of food, my stomach is starting to rumble," Carol admitted. "And the idea of oatmeal with applesauce is appealing."

"Sounds good to me."

"I'll get right to it." She stood.

"I just hope I don't get too used to being waited on by you." Maria chuckled.

Carol forced a smile but felt concerned. How would her aunt do on her own? She still didn't know Carol was leaving today. Mindful that the clock was ticking, Carol rechecked the weather forecast on her phone and then scanned the airline's website. The storm was predicted to worsen by evening, but she should be gone by then. No flights had gone out so far, but several were scheduled for early afternoon. Hers was still listed for an on-time departure.

She knew she should be relieved by this news as she read the oatmeal instructions. It wasn't like the instant packets she used at home. She measured water and salt and poured them into a saucepan. As she turned on the flame, she tried to imagine herself lazing in the Bahamas with Michigan and snowstorms far behind her. She should have been excited by the idea. Instead, she felt a heaviness at leaving Maria in the lurch like this.

As she got bowls out, she thought about Victor and how she'd enjoyed his company in the kitchen last night. Not to mention his culinary skills. And he was intelligent and kind and had a good sense of humor too. Of course, Maria's hint hadn't escaped her. And why shouldn't she want her only niece to marry her best friend's son? To a woman who confessed to enjoying Hallmark movies and rom-coms with happy endings, a match like that would be ideal, perhaps even "made in heaven."

But why was Carol being so silly? Why go there? Despite her aunt's gloomy forecast for Victor and Victoria, Carol wasn't convinced. Victor seemed too sincere to date a girl "for convenience." If he didn't have genuine interest in Victoria, why would he stick with her so long? Were good women in short supply around here? She smiled to herself, trying to blow this all off. She was thinking like a middle school girl.

She carefully measured the old-fashioned oats and poured them into the boiling water, just like the directions said. She turned on the timer, hoping the oatmeal mixture wouldn't stick to the pan or turn to glue. What kind of numbskull couldn't make oatmeal right? She chopped walnuts and even found a jar of raisins in the cupboard. Struggling to open the jar of applesauce, she imagined herself sitting outside her resort hotel, ordering whatever she liked from the menu and soaking in sun-shine while someone else fixed her breakfast. She imagined being catered to, returning to a comfortable room where her bed was not only made but turned down with a chocolate on the pillow. Just like in the brochure. She envisioned herself lounging by the pool or beach with a colorful, icy drink trimmed with a tiny paper parasol. Without a care in the world . . .

Except that she did have a care. She cared about Maria. They still hadn't figured out if her arm was really broken. She might need real help for a while. Carol couldn't help but care. And, as hard as it was to wrap her head around this, she cared about Victor too. She even cared about his family. Which seemed ridiculous since she hadn't even met Antonia and Larry. Yet she already felt pulled in. How had this happened in just twenty-four hours? It was like getting stuck here in Michigan had placed some kind of spell on her. She shook her head sharply, as if to dislodge the thoughts spinning around in there, but the stove timer went off, and she knew it was time to dish up the oatmeal and set the table.

She paused to read Maria's calendar by the door. Counting the days until Christmas, she saw it was less than a week away. Neatly penned in for the upcoming Saturday was "Habitat Fundraiser—Christmas Cotillion, 7:00 p.m." Victor had mentioned that yesterday. She scanned the calendar again, and saw "decorating for cotillion" penciled in for the two days before, reminding her that her aunt liked to help with that. Well, not this year.

Carol called out to Maria that breakfast was served, and soon they were both seated in the kitchen, bowing their heads while Maria asked a blessing. They both got quiet while eating. Carol was still trying to sort out her conflicting feelings. She'd only booked the Bahamas resort for a week, but already she'd lost one day. Even if she could extend her stay, it would be inconvenient since she'd promised Marsha she'd return after

Christmas to do the year-end inventory. Being stuck in the design firm's storage unit to count lamps and rugs and things sounded like a punishment right now. Especially if her Bahamas visit was ruined. Meanwhile, snowflakes were starting to fly outside the kitchen window again. Perhaps she'd be stuck here longer after all. Maybe that would be good. Or maybe she was just very confused.

7

As Carol loaded the dishwasher, Maria mentioned the upcoming Christmas Cotillion. "It's a historical dance that Miller's Creek has held every year since 1918. Well, except for those COVID years. That was very sad. We turned it into a fundraising event about twenty years ago. The last several years have been for Habitat for Humanity. I usually help out."

Carol noted the melancholy tone in her aunt's voice. "But you should be able to attend . . . I mean, your arm shouldn't keep you away, should it?" She put the detergent in the dishwasher dispenser, rinsed her hands, and turned to see Maria's downcast expression.

"Oh, yes, I'm sure I'll go," Maria said. "But I usually have such fun managing the decorations."

Carol re-hung the dish towel. "Why can't you still manage them? You did great directing Victor and me last night."

Maria smiled. "Well, you obviously knew what you were doing. But the cotillion is different." Her smile faded. "*Managing* is the wrong word. I usually do most of the legwork."

"Maybe this is your year to learn delegation." Carol refilled her coffee mug and briefly described how Marsha loved ordering her around at work. "You can just sit in a chair and tell everyone what to do."

Maria looked amused but unconvinced.

"I'd love to help if I could." Carol checked the kitchen clock, wishing she could pack more hours into the day. The least she could do would be help make her aunt's house Christmassy.

"No, no, I wouldn't expect that."

"How about if I get the rest of your house decorated today? We made some progress last night, but I know you're hosting friends and neighbors on Christmas Eve. Can I help you get the house all spruced up for that?"

Maria brightened. "Oh, Carol, I would absolutely love that. But what about your Christmas aversion? You sure you don't mind?"

Carol considered her answer. "Like I said, this is different. Decorating for you is nothing like doing it for some hoity-toity, hard-to-please client. Believe me."

"Well, I appreciate anything you can do. And I don't think I need to direct you. Unless you want me to."

"How about we collaborate?"

Maria lifted her mug in a toast. "Here's to collaboration."

After putting on *White Christmas* to amuse Maria, Carol spent an hour bringing down the rest of the boxes of decorations from the attic. By the time she was ready to begin, her aunt was snoozing in her recliner, still clutching her injured arm, but she looked peaceful enough that Carol hated to disturb her. Maybe this was for the best. She knew she could get more done if left to her own devices. And since Maria had seemed unconcerned—a refreshing change from paying clients with unrealistic expectations and goals to impress or outdo their family and friends—Carol wasn't worried.

In fact, with cheerful music from the movie playing in the background, it was surprisingly enjoyable. But she knew this was about to come to an end. If she wanted to make it to the airport, she'd need to leave the farm by 3:30. At least the weather seemed to be holding. A few flakes were flying and the sky was gray, but each time she gazed out over the beautiful snowy landscape, she was pleased to see no blizzard brewing. And according to her phone, her flight was still scheduled. But she still needed to secure some ground transportation. Not wanting to wake her snoozing aunt, she went up to her room to make these inquiries in private.

After several disappointing calls for Ubers and taxis, she knew it was useless. No one wanted to come way out to the farm just to drive her back to the city. They blamed everything from iffy weather to Christmastime. Realizing Victor might be her only hope, and that it was now past two, she called him. She couldn't hide the desperation in her voice as she spilled her woes, finally insisting she'd pay for his gas. But to her relief, he sounded happy to take her to the airport. Whether he was being a good neighbor or really needed to go to the city like he claimed, she couldn't tell. He might've just felt sorry for her.

Or perhaps he was just glad to see her go. She still grimaced remembering how she'd treated him on the ride out here. She'd been so full of herself and consumed by her worries that she'd probably offended him. And first impressions, she knew, tended to linger. Despite Victor's graciousness just now, he probably considered her pretty shallow. But as she packed her small carry-on, she thought of last night. Hadn't they gotten along well? Or was his help only for Maria's sake? Whatever the case, Victor promised to get her at 3:30, and he sounded confident they'd reach the airport on time for her flight.

Now to break the news to her aunt.

As she went down the stairs, she prepared her explanation. First, she would thank Maria for the hospitality, then she would tell her she hoped to come back to visit again when she had more time. And finally, she would tell her she had a flight going out early this evening. Maria was just waking up as Carol positioned herself in front of her chair. Clearing her throat, she made her awkward little speech. "Victor is giving me a ride," she said, wrapping up. "He'll be here within the hour."

"I suspected you were leaving." Maria's countenance faded. "But I do understand. I'm just glad to have had you as long as I did." Her eyes suddenly opened wide, and she waved her good hand toward the fully decorated mantel above the woodstove. "Oh my goodness." She paused and gazed around the room. "You're an absolute wonder. A decorating whiz. It's beautiful, Carol. Just beautiful!"

"Thanks. I was hoping you'd like it. I'm sure it's not how you'd normally dec—"

"No, it's not. It's way better. My word. It's stunning! Thank you so much for your hard work."

Carol was already gathering up the last of the emptied bins, nesting them into one large box. "I'm going to put these back in the attic with the rest of the boxes. Get them out of the way." Her heart felt lighter as she went back up the stairs. It was nice to get such genuine appreciation. Not at all like working for Marsha's clients. Finally, she straightened up the bedroom and bathroom she'd been using, changed into the traveling outfit she'd worn in Seattle, and then with carry-on in hand, went back down.

"Oh, Carol. You can't possibly wear that," Maria exclaimed when she saw her. "You'll worry me to death—and probably catch pneumonia."

Carol shrugged. "I'll be okay."

"No, no, no. You go put on jeans and a sweater *right now*. Before my old heart gives out. And you can wear my boots and parka to the airport. Send them back with Victor if you like, although I don't really care."

She complied with her aunt's command, then hurried back down, hoping to fix a light dinner for her aunt to enjoy that evening. She hurriedly scrounged around, finally putting a tuna sandwich and slices of apple and cheese on a plate she covered with plastic wrap. It wasn't much of a dinner, and she chided herself for not having offered to go to the grocery store today, but she'd been so caught up in decorating, it never occurred to her. She was just wiping down the kitchen countertops when she heard Victor's voice in the living room. To her surprise, it was almost 3:30. She grabbed Maria's parka and snow boots and hurried out.

"I put a plate with dinner in the fridge. It's not much." She turned to Victor. "I wish I'd thought to get her some groceries," she explained as she tugged on the boots.

"Looks like you were busy decorating," Victor said. "Nice work."

"Thanks."

"I'll get some supplies for you on my way back," he promised Maria, kissing her lightly on the cheek. "Maybe Carol can tell me what you need on the way to the airport."

"For sure." She nodded as she zipped the parka. "I really appreciate the ride, Victor." She turned to Maria, whose eyes glistened with tears.

"Oh, Aunt Maria." Carol leaned down to give her a clumsy hug. "I mean what I said earlier. I'd love to come back for a longer visit someday. I've had such a great time here . . . Getting to know you has been a wonderful surprise. I wouldn't trade my layover here for anything."

"Not even a sunny Bahamian beach?" Victor teased.

"Not even," Carol answered.

"Well, we better get going."

"You take care, Aunt Maria. Don't overdo it. And please consider getting your arm checked by a doctor." She kissed her aunt's cheek, then whispered, "I love you."

Maria's tears began to flow freely now, but she nodded, mouthing "I love you" back to Carol. "Thank you for everything," she said hoarsely.

"Thank you!" Carol said. "For everything."

"Send me a postcard from the Bahamas," Maria called out as Carol followed Victor to the door.

"I definitely will!" Carol blew a final kiss, then went outside, feeling hot tears stinging her eyes. She turned away from Victor as he took her bag and tossed it into the pickup bed. But when he opened the truck door for her, she tried to conceal her sadness by wiping her damp cheeks with the back of her hand.

They were well past town before Victor broke the silence between them.

"You and Maria seem to have hit it off." His tone was tentative, as if he'd noticed her tears, after all. The trouble was, she hadn't gotten hold of her emotions yet. She was still overwhelmed by a flood of confusing and conflicting feelings—building resentment toward her mom, guilt for leaving Maria in the lurch, sadness at departing from a home that felt more like a home than any she'd ever known.

Perhaps the last was most disturbing. Or maybe she was just feeling humiliated. She didn't want to admit—even to herself—that there was a lonely little girl still pining away for all she'd imagined she'd missed out on growing up. Good grief, she was almost forty. She should have gotten over it by now. *Move on!*

"I know she really appreciated your help, Carol." Victor's words interrupted her thoughts. "It was amazing what you did during such a short—"

"Stop it!" she blurted out, breaking into fresh sobs. "I-I'm sorry. I didn't mean to say that."

"No, no." His tone was soothing. "It's okay. I think I get it."

"*I* don't even get it," she choked out. "I-I wish I-I hadn't abandoned her. Not like that! She *needs* me." She sobbed. "And—and—I need her too." She was crying harder now. And it was an ugly cry too. She went on blubbering and nearly choked when she tried to stop. She was crying so hard, it was painful. Turning from him, she attempted to breathe and inwardly scolded herself for being so juvenile. She tried to calm herself by staring out at the peaceful snowscape all around, but nothing worked. Like a bad Seattle rain, the tears kept falling.

Something light landed on her lap, and she turned to see a neatly folded red bandanna there. She choked out a gruff thank-you, then used it to blot her wet face. She took some slow, deep breaths, trying to compose herself enough to speak.

"I, uh, I don't usually fall apart like that," she said quietly. "In fact, I can't remember ever doing that before."

"It's okay," he repeated. "I think I get it."

"Really? Then can you please explain it to me?"

He chuckled. "Okay, I'll try." He shared more about the difficult era when his heart got broken by the woman he'd planned to marry. "I threw myself into my restaurant, gave it everything I had—time, money, energy. And I know it takes that kind of devotion to make a restaurant work, but it wasn't healthy."

She nodded. In a weird way, she understood.

"During the COVID shutdowns, I started having anxiety attacks and, later on, I think it morphed into depression. I blamed it on the money I was losing from forced closures, but looking back now, I know it was because I wasn't crazy-busy like I'd been before. I had too much time to think . . . to deal with repressed feelings . . . to admit I'd been in denial."

"Uh-huh." She nodded, afraid to admit that sounded way too familiar.

"So anyway, when I heard Mom needed help with Dad, it felt like a sign that I needed to let the restaurant go." He shook his head. "But it wasn't easy. Vittorio's was all I had. Or so it seemed. Like a dog with a bone, I wouldn't let it go, even if a T-bone steak was waiting for me."

"Living with your parents is a T-bone steak?"

"Surprisingly, yes. At first it seemed like a sacrifice, you know, to give up my dream. But it felt like the right thing to do." He let out a long sigh. "A few months after I moved back, I was out on the tractor. It was a sunny spring day. Everything was coming up green and smelling fresh and clean, and it just hit me. I was *home*." He shrugged. "And out there, discing the alfalfa field, I started to just bawl like a great, big baby. I thought I was crying about losing my restaurant, but then I realized I was crying for my mom and my dad . . . and for being there when they needed me. It felt good to be needed like that. It felt good to be home."

"Wow," she said under her breath. "I think you do understand."

"Yeah . . . and just for the record, I never told that story to anyone before, but I figure you're safe since you're leaving the country." His laugh was stiff.

"I won't repeat your story," she promised, frowning at the heavy gray sky lurking ahead. "Sure looks dark out there. Does the sun go down this early?"

"Not this early. Looks like bad weather. Have you checked your flight lately? You sure everything's still on time? We're not that far from Grand Rapids, and that storm looks pretty thick in that direction." He pointed ahead. "And snow's starting up again."

"I should've gotten a text or email if my flight was canceled." She tugged her phone from her bag only to discover it was dead. She had been so focused on spending her last day with her aunt that she forgot to charge it. "I don't suppose you have a charger cord in here?"

"I keep meaning to get one, but it has to plug into the cigarette lighter with this old truck. Not easy to find."

"Radio?" she tried.

"We can do better." He reached into his coat pocket. "Use mine. Although connection can be patchy." He told her his passcode, but it took a while to connect.

They were just outside the city, and it was nearly whiteout conditions when she got online. She pulled up her flight info and deflated. "It says it's delayed," she told him. "I'll check my email."

"Well, no point going to the airport before you know for sure." Victor pulled into a parking lot while they waited.

"Yep, I got an update," she announced. "My flight is officially canceled."

"You don't seem too disappointed." He sounded surprised.

She considered her feelings. "Honestly, I think I'm relieved."

He grinned at her. "Me too."

"And you know what?" She broke into a big smile. "I've made up my mind."

"About?"

"I'm canceling the whole thing—my whole trip. It's just not worth it. And now I can spend more time at Maria's. I can help her." She felt like a huge weight had been lifted. "Even if I lose money on my cancelation, I don't care. It just feels right."

"Good for you."

A wave of guilt rushed over her. "But I made you drive all this way and now it looks like another blizzard."

He put the pickup in reverse and cautiously pulled back onto the street. "Like I told you, I needed to come. I have to stop by my old restaurant." His wiper blades slid back and forth to keep the windshield clear.

She was skeptical. Was he just being nice? "Why did you need to go *today*?"

"The owners keep reminding me about some boxes I have in the storage room. I keep forgetting, and just this week they threatened to throw them out if I didn't get them before the year's end."

"So you really needed to go specifically today?" she repeated herself.

"Well, today or someday between now and the thirty-first. Now seemed as good a time as ever. Kill two birds with one stone as my dad used to say."

She was pretty sure he'd only come in order to help her, but she appreciated it nonetheless. "Well, I'd love to see your old restaurant. Is it still called Vittorio's?"

"No, I insisted on keeping the name for myself, along with the signage and menus and things. I have them stored in the barn at home. Just in case I ever restart things."

"Do you want to?"

"Maybe someday. But not in the city. I think I'm done with that. Maybe in Miller's Creek. A smaller version, anyway."

"Maria is hoping you'll do that. She said she'd be a regular patron."

"Bless Maria." He turned up the truck's heater.

She nodded, still feeling a little teary over how close she'd come to leaving her aunt this evening. At least she had a few more days now. She felt God had a firm hand in all this and, as Victor navigated the snowy streets through town, she silently prayed a sincere thank-you for allowing her to come "home." Oh, she knew Miller's Creek wasn't truly her home, but it would feel like it for a while longer. At least until Christmas.

8

Snow was falling hard by the time Victor parked in front of a brick building with lights glowing inside. "Is this Vittorio's?" Carol asked.

"Well, like I mentioned, I kept my name so it's no longer Vittorio's." He pointed to the neon "Paolo's Pizzeria" sign in the front window that was only slightly obscured by snow. "It shouldn't take me long to get my boxes. You can stay in the pickup if you want to keep warm and dry. I can leave the engine running and heater on."

"How about if I help you?" she suggested. "I'd love to see inside the restaurant. It looks charming."

"It used to be," he said dourly.

Sensing this wasn't easy for him, she didn't comment. Instead, she got out and jogged behind him through the blowing snow. A bell tinkled as they entered, but the small restaurant had only one table of customers, a family of four who were sharing a pizza.

"Smells good," she whispered to him.

"Yeah." He barely nodded, then called out to the guy behind the counter. "I'm here for the boxes from Vittorio's you've been storing for me."

The man jerked his thumb over a shoulder. "In the office, by the door."

She followed him down a dark hallway and into a messy room that slightly resembled an office. "That's them." Victor pointed to three storage boxes. "If you can manage one, I can get the other two."

She thrust her arms out for him to set the box on. "So, how's their pizza here?"

"I don't really know." He lifted the other two boxes with a grunt and pushed the door open with one foot.

"You've never even tried it?"

"No. I guess maybe I was treating it like sour grapes." His smile was crooked.

"Well, I'm hungry, and it smells good. Plus it's a long drive back to the farm."

"Maybe we should give Paolo's a try."

"Looks like he could use the business."

They went back to the storefront and ordered a medium mushroom and Italian sausage pizza, then took the boxes out to the pickup, where she helped him fight against the wind. Together they wrapped the boxes in a plastic tarp to protect them from the weather. Back inside, they removed their coats, shook off the snow, and sat down at a small table.

He patted the laminate tabletop. "I got these fixtures for a good deal," he told her. "They're not much to look at, but I always put red-and-white gingham tablecloths on them. And then I topped them with an old-fashioned wine bottle with dripping candle wax."

"Just like *Lady and the Tramp*," she declared.

He laughed. "Exactly my inspiration."

She lowered her voice. "Is it hard to be here?"

He shrugged. "A little. But I guess it's good therapy. Thanks for pushing me. I probably needed it."

"Well, the building itself is charming. I love the old wood

floors and stucco walls. And the iron lanterns are a nice old-world touch. I can imagine how charming it used to be."

"Yeah, I never had that long counter over there or the soda machine. Or those big pizza signs, of course." He frowned. "I had these great vintage travel posters of Italy in nice frames. In fact, I still have them. And I used to have a lot of big plants, but I left them behind." He glanced around. "I'm guessing they bit the dust." He sighed. "I always tried to create an atmosphere that made customers feel like they were somewhere else . . . or maybe even that they'd gone back in time."

"I would've liked a place like that." She smiled. "Especially if the food was good."

His brows arched as if he was about to defend his culinary skills.

She beat him to it. "And I know your food would've been excellent."

"Thank you." He sipped his water, then wrinkled his nose. "And I never used plastic glasses or dishes or anything like that." He pointed to the napkin dispenser. "And I always used cloth napkins. When I was starting out, I'd take linens home to launder myself."

"Very domestic," she teased.

"Mostly just cheap." He paused as the pizza was set down, along with two plastic plates. He thanked the server, then bowed his head to say a short but sincere blessing.

They got quiet as they began to eat. Although Carol was hungry, she was a bit disappointed by the pizza. "I think it smelled better than it tastes," she whispered to him. "Kinda validates your low opinion, if that makes you feel any better."

"Well, in Paul's defense—that's the owner—this weather has probably taken its toll on traffic. Maybe he's not into pizza-making tonight."

"Yes. I'm surprised he's even open."

"Right. Maybe it's an off night."

She took another bite, slowly chewing the tough crust. It was crispy on the outside but doughy and undercooked in the middle.

"Tell me about your life back in Seattle," he said, using a plastic fork to scrape off the pizza topping that he proceeded to eat, leaving the gummy crust behind.

She followed his example, then tried to think of a way to describe her life back in Seattle. It suddenly seemed so far away and removed, like it was another world. Maybe it was. "Well, I mostly just work. I mean, I have a few friends that I socialize with, but sometimes I'll work so hard staging a house for a realtor that I come home exhausted and just flop down with a frozen dinner and an old movie. I guess I've gotten into something of a rut."

"Do you enjoy your work?"

She thought he already knew the answer to this but decided to fill him in a little more, painting an even gloomier picture.

"And the Seattle weather? What's it like? All I've heard is that it rains a lot."

"It definitely rains. But on a clear day, it's beautiful there." She sighed. "But clear days seem few and far between."

"And you don't really have family there?"

"Family?" She pursed her lips. "I honestly don't know that I've ever had family. Not really." She began to pour out her story . . . about a lonely little girl whose parents fought like cats and dogs, then split up. She painted a tale about a preoccupied single mom, more interested in dating than parenting. "To put it mildly, my mom was not a homemaker. I guess that's why I got so interested in home decor and why I was so thrilled to get a place of my own and make it beautiful . . . and homey."

"So your place is homey?"

She considered this. "Well, it's attractive enough. But homey? To be honest, I don't think so. Not like Maria's house is homey. But when I furnished it, I suppose I was thinking more about impressing others than I was about my own comfort or coziness. And then I got so busy with work, I never really got around to making it look the way I wanted."

"Guess that's city life, eh?"

"I guess." She considered this. "But you know, if I were to have my own design firm, I'd like to make it more about cozy comfort than style and money. A way to make home a home. In college I used to imagine a way to incorporate the kind of beauty that God put in the natural world all around us into the design of a home." She frowned at her old unrealistic dream. "But even if I could figure out how to do that, I doubt I'd have any customers."

"Why not? That seems like a great business plan to me. Imitating God's beautiful creation, making people comfortable in their own homes—what could be better?"

"I agree . . . in theory. But it seems the ones looking for design help have one goal in mind . . . okay, make that two." She held up a forefinger. "Spend money." Another finger. "Impress friends."

"That's pretty sad."

"I agree."

"But I bet you could find customers who prefer a homey home."

She was skeptical. "I don't know."

"Around here, you could. I'm sure of it. Don't give up on your dream, Carol."

"Well, it's just a dream . . . I doubt I'll ever achieve it."

He waved a hand, gesturing around the restaurant. "This was just a dream for me. Well, not *this* . . . but the way I had it *before*."

"But you gave it up."

He nodded grimly. "Yeah. For family."

"Right."

"But the dream is still in me. Really, I'm not done yet. And neither are you." He picked up his plastic cup. "Here's to dreams."

"To dreams." She clicked hers against his . . . wondering.

* * * *

The drive back to the farm was quiet. Partly because Carol didn't want to distract Victor from his focus on the road. The truck's grip on the slippery streets seemed precarious, and he was being so careful, she didn't want to be to blame if they wound up in the ditch or behind a tow truck, like some of the vehicles they'd seen.

Finally, when he was turning down Maria's driveway, she spoke. "I really am relieved not to be flying to the Bahamas, after all."

"You really don't mind giving up those sunny beaches?"

"Not really. Being with my aunt is a good trade."

"I know Maria will be thrilled to have you."

"And I hope I can help more around the house. And maybe even with the cotillion decorations. I know how important that is to her. She seemed really worried that no one would step up."

"You'd be the perfect candidate." He chuckled. "Well, if you can keep setting aside your negative attitude toward Christmas."

"I'm working on it."

"Who knows? By the time you leave Michigan, you might even like the holidays. If Maria has any influence, she might transform your Grinchy thoughts completely."

"Well, don't expect miracles."

He pulled up next to the house but kept the engine running. "We'll all do everything we can to make sure your Christmas is the best one ever."

Her smile was tolerant as she remembered her past Christmases and how bleak most had been. "Well, that shouldn't be a big challenge."

He used a bandanna to wipe humidity from his side window. "Now, if you're going to help decorate for the cotillion, there's no time to waste. You do know it's scheduled for Saturday night? But Maria usually just puts up the same decorations every year so it shouldn't be too difficult."

"Unless I could make it more special." She wondered how that would even be possible. Or if people would appreciate it if she did. Small town folks might be resistant to change. "I'd like to see the venue where the event is held and what kind of decorations they use."

"It's in the Miller's Creek Grange Hall each year, and I'm sure Maria can tell you where everything is stored. Although I doubt she can be of much physical help."

Carol reached for the passenger side door handle, then paused. "I really feel Maria should get her arm checked. And probably x-rayed too. I'm worried it's more than just a sprain, and she could have permanent damage if it heals badly."

"I've had the same concern. How about I pick you two up in the morning? It can be under the guise of taking you to check out the decorating biz at the Grange. Maria will gladly agree to that. But then after she shows you around a bit, I can escort her over to urgent care."

"Perfect. And if necessary, I will use my decoration assistance as leverage. I can refuse to help her if she refuses to get her arm looked at."

"Great idea!" He hopped out of the pickup and trudged through the snow to open her door, helping her out, then catching her as her boot slid on the slick driveway.

"Whoa," he said, holding her close until she was able to steady herself. "You almost did a face-plant there."

"Thank you." She stepped back self-consciously.

He grabbed her bag, and she hurried up to the porch, then thanked him again. "For everything," she told him. "It's been a surprisingly pleasant evening."

"I agree." He tipped his cowboy hat. "See you in the morning."

Carol found her aunt snoozing in her recliner with her partially eaten dinner on the TV tray next to her. Although she hated to disturb her, Carol felt like Maria would rest better in her own bed. She gently nudged her aunt's good arm and soon, blinking in surprise, Maria smiled. "Am I dreaming or are you still here?"

"I came back." Carol winked. "Just like a bad penny."

"More like a *lucky* penny." Maria reached out with her good hand, grasping Carol's fingers and giving them a squeeze. "I'm so glad you did."

Carol gently removed the afghan from her aunt's lap, then helped her to her feet. "Just in time to tuck you in bed too." As she helped her aunt with her nighttime routine, Carol told her about the canceled flight, her choice to remain throughout Christmas, and the pizza she'd shared with Victor.

"That's wonderful." Maria set her toothbrush back in the holder. "The best Christmas present anyone could give me."

By the time Carol got Maria into her bed, she had presented the plan for Victor to take them to the Grange first thing in the morning. "I want to see about decorating for the cotillion since it's right around the corner. But I thought you'd want to go too." She tucked the soft quilt up by Maria's chin. "To direct me, you know, like you did with the Christmas tree."

Maria chuckled. "As I recall I slept while you and Victor decorated for me."

Carol smiled. "Well, I'd still appreciate your input and suggestions."

"Of course, dear. I wouldn't miss it."

Carol leaned down to kiss her aunt's cheek, wishing her sweet dreams. Maria assured her that she would have nothing but now that Carol was back.

Satisfied that she'd made the right decision to give up on the

Bahamas, Carol picked up her aunt's dinner dishes, straightened up the kitchen, checked the thermostat, and turned off the lights. When she finally went up to her room, she plugged her phone into the charger, then canceled her resort reservation and booked a return flight to Seattle after Christmas.

Then, realizing it was late and that she needed to get up early to complete some chores for Maria, she contentedly unpacked her meager bag and prepared for bed. Being here, even for just a week, felt almost magical to her. Perhaps Victor was right. Maybe she really would learn to see Christmas in a fresh new light and finally appreciate the holiday for what it was meant to be: a celebration of the One who'd come to give the world hope. Because that was how she felt as she drifted off to sleep . . . hopeful.

9

Carol was sound asleep when her phone began to jangle loudly. Getting her bearings, she found her phone and checked the time. It was well past midnight. Who would call at this hour? According to her caller ID, it was her mom. This could be a record—two conversations with her mother within the same week? She unplugged the charger and answered groggily.

"Hi, honey bunches." Mom sounded uncharacteristically bright and cheerful. Had she been drinking? "How's the Bahamas? Sunny and warm, I bet." She chattered on before Carol could respond. "Anyway, I decided to join you down there, sweetie. I've just started to pack my bags and couldn't choose which swimsuit to pack and thought I'd call you to see if you'd be too embarrassed to see your poor old mother in a bikini. I have to admit, I don't look half bad."

Carol wondered if she was having a nightmare. "Do you know what time it is?"

"I think it's around nine, maybe ten. I didn't really check to—"

"It's approaching one in the morning here."

"Oh, sorry. Time difference. Well, anyway, aren't you excited to spend time together in the Bahamas?"

Carol sat up, trying to arrange the right words but nothing came. Did her mom really expect to meet in the Bahamas?

"Ed is driving me up a wall," Mom shared. "Honestly, he's just a big old grump. Worse than the Grinch who stole Christmas. I told him if he didn't treat me better, I'd leave him to run away with my daughter and he didn't even care. He said to go ahead and go, so I was searching flights out of Phoenix, and I found a seat for tomorrow night and—"

"I'm not in the Bahamas, Mom. I'm still in Michigan." Carol leaned back against the soft bed. "And like I said, it's rather late here, so if you don't mind—"

"Why on earth are you still there? In the Michigan sticks of all places? *Seriously*?"

Carol quickly explained the situation. "So I just decided to give up on the Bahamas altogether. I plan to stay on here through the holidays."

"Are you kidding? You'd give up the beach for that?"

Carol tried to sound more patient than she felt as she explained about staying at Maria's house, about the injured arm, and how Maria needed help. But the other end of the line remained dead silent. Crickets.

"Mom?" She cleared her throat. "Are you still there?"

"Maria can just find someone else to be her handmaid." Mom's tone grew sharper. "You get yourself to the Bahamas, Carol Louise. First thing tomorrow. I will meet you there the next day—"

"I already canceled the whole works, Mom. I'm not going—"

"Why on earth would you give that up? The Bahamas for Maria's old farmhouse? It's perfectly ridiculous."

"I *like* being here. Maria is family."

"Family? Seriously?" Her mom made a strangled-sounding laugh. "Trust me, Maria is *not* family."

"She's your sister."

"Only by blood. Bad blood too!"

"I don't get that, Mom. Maria is so sweet. Why do you refuse to even—"

"Maria is selfish and—"

"I don't think you really know her."

"Ha! I know her better than anyone. Don't you understand that she abandoned me when I was a young child? She was much older, and she was supposed to take care of me after our mom died. Dad even paid her to do it. But she was so selfish. She just left me to live alone with our father like I was nothing to her. And he was a monster, Carol! Always drunk and abusive. It was a horrible place for a child to be. No, Maria is *not* family! And if you're helping her, you're not family either."

Carol sat up again, fully awake now. "You never told me any of that. I mean, you said Poppy drank some, but you said he always worked and supported you. Sure, you told me about being lonely, but you always said how he was basically a good man, how you never went without anything. And you never mentioned any kind of abuse." Carol thought this might explain why her mother's parenting was the way it was—bordering on abusive and certainly neglectful. Or else she was flat-out lying. And it wouldn't be the first time.

"I wanted to spare you from the sordid details of my youth."

Carol rolled her eyes at her mom's characteristically melodramatic remarks. Guilt-tripping her daughter was her favorite MO for acquiring sympathy and getting her way.

"Maria ran off and got married to some old man. And he was a perfect stranger too. She didn't even introduce him to us. Just snuck off in the middle of the night. She abandoned your poppy and me, left us all alone to fend for ourselves. That's probably why he started to drink more heavily. Really, honey, that woman is totally selfish and self-centered, and it's unforgivable that she's now guilting you into remaining with her. But you're an adult! Tell her to forget it! That you've decided to spend your holidays with your own mother. It's your choice, Carol."

"The weather didn't give me much of a choice, Mom. And, honestly, I had no idea you wanted to go to the Bahamas with me. I'm sorry."

"But I'm telling you that now. Aren't you listening?"

"It's too late. Like I said, I already canceled everything."

"Well, *un-cancel* everything."

"I can't."

"Or you won't? I can't believe it. You're choosing that selfish woman over the mother who raised you? What an ungrateful child I suffered and sacrificed for—"

"Mom." Carol couldn't hide her exasperation at her mom's dramatic efforts. She was familiar with the guilt-inducing manipulation her mother utilized to her own benefit. "No offense, but the way you raised me wasn't ideal. I mean, you wouldn't exactly have won any mommy of the year awards."

Unsurprisingly, this was followed by a dramatic gasp from her mother. "This is just fine! My own child turning on me. Maria ruined my childhood and now she's ruining my Christmas plans to be with my daughter too."

"Really? Your *plans*? This sounds pretty last minute to me. You sure you really wanted to be with me?" Carol thought her mother was more likely trying to punish her husband by running away and Carol provided a handy escape.

"Oh, Carol. You know that we never get to spend quality time together. You're always working, and I'm getting old. Who knows how many more holidays I have left?" Now her voice turned to honey. "And, for the record, I happen to enjoy my daughter's company. After all, you're a beautiful, intelligent woman. I'm always bragging about my girl to my friends—how you put yourself through college and your impressive career in the design business. You're so independent, living on your own in the big city."

Carol was used to the guilt trips, but this sugary flattery was a new twist. Was it sincere or manipulative? Was she being too hard on her mother? Maybe she really did miss her. "If you really do want to be with me, I'm sure Maria would welcome you here. Her house is lovely. There's plenty of room, and I'd love to—"

"I would rather be starved than spend my Christmas with *that* woman, thank you very much! And if that's what you plan to do, I'm cutting you off as my daughter!" Then the line went silent.

Carol set her phone down and sighed. It was always difficult to sort out her feelings after a conversation with her mother, but this one took the cake. And now, instead of feeling hopeful and happy about her holiday plans, she felt guilty and confused, followed by hurt and angry. And she knew getting back to sleep would be a challenge.

* * * *

After a restless night's sleep, Carol was still simmering over the late-night conversation as she looked out her window into the gray dawn light. The snow outside was even deeper now. Perhaps three feet, though she wasn't sure. Knowing she'd need to dig firewood out of the snow, she decided to dress warmly. As she tugged on layers of her aunt's loaner clothing, she wondered if there was any truth to her mom's claims last night. The accusations against Poppy, the blame she laid on her sister, not to mention this sudden unexpected longing to spend time together. Was any of it real? Would Carol ever know? Did she really care that her mother was disowning her? It's not like they'd ever been close.

Despite her attempts to block out these questions, they were still tumbling through her head as she went downstairs. The house was quiet. She peeked in Maria's bedroom and was glad to see her aunt sleeping peacefully. As she tiptoed to the kitchen to make coffee, she wondered if she should tell Maria about her mom's accusations. If they were true, it would be very awkward, to say the least. And if they were manufactured, it would only hurt her aunt's feelings. Maybe it was better to let sleeping dogs lie. Or narcissistic mothers lie. Anyway, if she did decide to bring it up to her aunt, she saw no need to hurry.

* * * *

Shortly after Carol got her morning chores completed, and she and Maria finished breakfast, Victor showed up to take them to town, first letting Carol into the cab, then gently helping Maria. Although she said nothing, Carol could see her aunt's face twisting in pain as he buckled her seat belt.

"Sorry to be slow in getting here," he told them as he got in. "I had to catch up with plowing some of the farmers' roads. It really piled up last night."

Carol turned to her aunt. "Do you think this weather will affect your Christmas Cotillion?"

"Oh, this is Michigan farm country, honey." Maria laughed. "It'd take more than a little snow to keep folks away."

"At least the major roads have been plowed," Victor said as he turned onto the main highway. "And the forecast for the next few days is sunny."

"Perfect." Maria winced slightly as they went over a big lump of snow.

"Still having a lot of pain there?" Victor asked.

"Oh, I don't know . . ." Maria looked down at her arm, bundled against her beneath her oversized parka. "I guess it takes time."

"She's still experiencing a lot of pain," Carol told him. "I made sure she took something for it with her breakfast to help her on the ride."

"Well, my mom and I both think she needs to pay a visit to urgent care," Victor said.

"Maybe in time," Maria told him. "After a few more days."

"Nope," he retorted. "It could be healing badly by then. Mom said to take you to urgent care this morning."

"This morning?" Maria was clearly alarmed. "But I have to help Carol—"

"You can explain where you store the cotillion decorations as we drive," Victor told her.

"But I need to show her where to—"

"I can show her," Victor interrupted again. "I know the Grange as well as anyone. Good grief, I grew up there. As kids we used to play hide-and-seek in that old building. I know it inside and out."

Maria's eyes looked glassy. "But I should—"

"You should get your arm looked at." Carol interrupted this time. "I'm sure Victor and I will do fine on our own."

"Besides, Mom told me I couldn't take you to the Grange until you got your arm looked at," Victor said. "So there's no point arguing, unless you don't care if the decorations get put up this year."

Maria slumped against her seat. "So I'm being kidnapped."

Victor laughed. "Well, I guess you could say that."

As they drove to town, Maria handed over her Grange key and explained where the decorations were stored. It all sounded pretty simple and straightforward. Carol asked a few questions, just to make her aunt feel more involved and perhaps instill a bit more confidence in her capabilities. Before long, Victor was pulling up to a big barnlike structure. "This is it." He slid out of the cab so Carol could exit through the driver's side, leaving the engine running and the heater going.

"I'll give her the quick tour and be right back," he promised Maria. "You stay put—or else."

As they trudged through the snow, up to the side door Maria had said to use, Carol thanked him. "That was a brilliant idea to entice Maria to cooperate."

"Thanks! I'll get her all checked into urgent care, then come back to help you. I'm guessing she'll be tied up for at least a couple hours."

Once inside, Victor turned on the overhead fluorescent lights, then led her to the storage closet Maria had told them about. It wasn't hard to spot the boxes clearly marked "Christmas Cotillion."

Carol tugged out a box, peeked inside, and saw sparkling garlands. "Looks pretty straightforward to me."

He pointed out where some folded tables, ladders, and other helpful items were stored, then turned up the heat and wished her good luck.

"You're probably the one who needs that with Maria," she joked.

He tipped his cowboy hat and grinned. "Well, we got her over a barrel. No cooperation at the hospital means no decoration happens here."

After he left, Carol set up a couple of folding tables and began removing boxes from the storage room. She opened each one to evaluate what she had to work with and estimate how much time and effort this might take. Some of the decorations had definitely seen better days and, since there were far more than necessary, she set some boxes aside to be returned to the storage room. She retrieved a borrowed notepad from her bag, then took a few minutes to study the layout of the large room. She began to sketch out a plan of sorts. Though she had no idea what her aunt or anyone else would think of the final product, it looked pretty good to her. She was just going for the ladder when Victor returned.

"Sorry that took so long," he apologized as he removed his fleece-lined jacket and cowboy hat. "What can I do?"

She showed him her sketches, explaining how she planned to execute the whole thing.

"Wow, you're really organized," he said as he set the ladder up near the small stage like she'd instructed.

"Well, time's a-wasting," she said as she carried a box of garlands over to him. "And we might not get a full day's work in today. Maria might need to go home to rest after they tend to her arm."

"I had the same thought. Plus, I promised Mom I'd stop by the grocery store."

"We could use groceries too." She handed him the end of an evergreen garland. "Attach that in the center next to that light strip, please." She squinted. "Those fluorescent lights sure are bright. Do they usually leave them on during the dance?"

"Can't really remember for sure. But I think so."

"Seems it'd be nicer to have softer lighting. Make it feel warmer and cozier."

"I'm sure you're right but not sure how you'd accomplish that." He stretched to hold up the garland. "How's that look?"

"Great." She grinned, wondering if she was referring to the garland or how handsome he looked perched up on the ladder in his Wranglers and plaid flannel shirt. She glanced away, resuming her focus. That kind of ogling was so out of character for her.

For the next hour or so, they worked together happily. And besides taking her direction surprisingly well, Victor even contributed a few creative suggestions of his own. The results were promising. "At this rate, I'm sure we'll have everything ready in time for the dance," she told him as she set an emptied box aside.

He glanced at his watch. "I don't know about you, but I'm ready for a coffee break."

"It's like you're reading my mind," she said.

"If you feel like a little walk, there's one fairly close by."

Once they were bundled up again, they headed outside where the sun was shining against a clear blue sky. "Oh, wow, it's so beautiful out here." She blinked against the light.

"Sunshine on snow really brightens things up."

"So cheerful." She tugged a new pair of sunglasses from her bag, ones she'd purchased for the Bahamas. "And it reminds me of my question for the cotillion. If we could round up some table and floor lamps, it would really improve the ambiance in there during the event."

"I'm sure my mom would be glad to loan you some, and Maria could probably contribute some too."

"I don't think it'd take too many. I thought about candles, but that might be a fire hazard. Of course, we could get electric candles." She glanced down the street. "Do you guys have a dollar store?"

He pointed a thumb over his shoulder. "Just a block beyond Java Jump Shot—that's where we're going."

"Handy."

10

They ordered to-go coffees and were soon pushing a squeaky cart through the dollar store. In the seasonal section, Carol browsed and then, feeling like she'd won the Michigan lottery, held up a small red-enamel lantern, testing to see that the golden flickering light actually worked. "Look at all these cute things. We could put one on each table." She picked up a small wreath of faux greens and fruit trimmed with a cheery plaid bow. Holding it horizontally in one hand, she placed the lantern in the center. "See? This could be a centerpiece. I'll put one on each table."

He looked a bit uncertain. "Uh-huh . . ."

She eagerly picked up another decoration. "A lot of these pieces really lend themselves to the motif I'm trying to achieve."

His brow creased slightly. "What *motif* is that?"

She grinned and playfully poked his arm. "You mean you can't see it?"

He grimaced. "Not exactly."

"Well, it's probably a bit on the nose, but I'm thinking old-fashioned country Christmas. You know, like the olden days, with lots of country chic charm, like patchwork quilts and lanterns and canning jars and other sweet, homey things. Maybe an antique or two borrowed from Maria's house. I just wish I had an electric fireplace or a woodstove we could use near the entrance with one of Maria's braided rugs."

He nodded like he was catching her vision now. "Okay, I get it. And I just happen to have an electric fireplace stored in the barn. It's got an old-world look. I used it in my restaurant in the wintertime to keep the chill off."

"That sounds absolutely perfect!" She put more items in their cart. "Can we borrow it?"

"Of course." He grinned.

She clapped with the excitement of a child, then threw her arms around him. "Thank you, thank you! It's all going to look great."

She was surprised by her unexpected display of affection but even more surprised that he returned her hug with enthusiasm. And that it felt nice! But suddenly he stiffened, and his arms dropped to his sides. She stepped back self-consciously. "Excuse my enthusiasm, but pulling all this together is a lot more fun than I expected." She tried to read his expression. Clearly, she'd made him uncomfortable. "I, uh, I'm surprised we haven't heard from urgent care yet." She fumbled to extract her phone from her pocket, pretending to focus on it but obsessing over his strange reaction just now.

"Hey, there, Victor," a very feminine voice cooed from behind Carol.

"Victoria." Victor's response sounded stiff. "What're you doing here?"

"Good point. I don't *usually* shop at the dollar store." The woman's tone sounded slightly arrogant. She laughed lightly. "But I saw you and your, uh, friend coming in here, and I thought I'd pop in and say hey. So what's up, old man? The dollar store doesn't seem like your usual haunt either."

Carol slowly turned, forcing an awkward smile as she put on her polite business veneer. "You must be Victoria Snyder," she said pleasantly, extending a hand. "I'm Maria's niece, Carol. Nice to meet you."

Victoria submitted to a weak handshake, then tipped her head to one side. "So what are you two doing in here?"

"Carol was looking for electric candles." For some reason he quickly segued to explaining Maria's injury, but while he rambled, Carol took a fast inventory of Victoria's appearance. Hollywood pretty in that fashionable blue-eyed blond sort of way, and her well-coordinated and probably expensive winter wear looked like something you'd see in Aspen. Although, Carol noted, it didn't look sturdy enough for skiing.

"In fact, we probably need to go check on her in urgent care right now," Victor told Victoria. "She's been there for several hours." He nodded to Carol. "We were scouting decorations for the cotillion since Carol has stepped in for her aunt."

Carol blinked, trying to think of an intelligent response. "That's right."

Now Victoria turned her attention from Victor to Carol with a slight frown. "The dollar store for cotillion decorations? That's a new twist. I thought the old ladies liked a rather traditional style. Are you sure they'll approve?" She picked up a lantern and dangled it over a finger with a pearly manicured nail, her brows arching with disapproval. "This is, uh, *interesting*."

The put-down was obvious but, not about to roll over, Carol stood straighter. "Well, I guess you have to use your imagination."

"I *imagine* you do." She let out another uppity laugh. "I'm surprised they gave you a budget. I don't want to burst your bubble, but those old Grange girls can be pretty conservative, not to mention tight with their purse strings."

Carol attempted what sounded like a rather phony laugh. "Well, I'm happy to donate these as my contribution to the dance. The dollar store is surprisingly affordable."

"I must agree they do carry some cheap merchandise."

Victoria's smile looked superior, or maybe it was victorious, as she linked her arm with Victor's and began to lead him away. "Speaking of Cotillion, Mr. Clarkson, we need to talk. Outside, if you don't mind. The aroma in here gives me a major headache."

Victor looked slightly trapped but he didn't pull away.

"You go on ahead," Carol told him. "I'll pay for these." She smiled, but as she wheeled the cart to the front of the store, she felt slightly shaken. She wasn't quite sure why. Oh, sure, the put-down wasn't nice, but she knew people back in Seattle who acted like that all the time. She suspected she felt somewhat territorial over Victor. But what right did she have to feel that way? And, really, what was the big deal? She already knew that he was involved with this Victoria character. Carol thought she understood why her aunt didn't care for the woman, but what was it to Carol if Victor liked Victoria? Suddenly, it hit her. Those two names together almost seemed as if their union were written in stone. Of course, why hadn't that occurred to her before? *Victor and Victoria* . . . they went together like coffee and donuts, sugar and cream, peanut butter and jelly . . . war and peace.

"Can I help you?" a young woman with lime green hair and a tattoo running around her whole neck asked.

"Yes." Carol fumbled to set her items on the conveyor belt, and the girl rang them up. She had just finished paying when she received a call from an unknown number. The cashier bagged her multitude of random purchases, while an urgent care nurse let Carol know that Maria was ready to be picked up. Promising they'd be there as soon as possible and, with loaded bags in hand, Carol hurried out to tell Victor.

"Don't forget what I said," Victoria called out sweetly as Victor took some of Carol's bags. They headed back toward the Grange.

"Sorry to interrupt," Carol told him.

He assured her it was no problem and then mumbled something about pulling the pickup around. Then he took off, leaving her with the bags. Feeling somewhat abandoned and weirdly dismayed, she watched him run down the recently shoveled sidewalk, hoping he wouldn't slip and fall.

Neither spoke as Victor drove them to the other side of town. By the time Carol could think of anything to say, he was pulling into the urgent care parking lot. "What about locking up the Grange?" she blurted out as he parked right next to the entrance.

"I locked it," he informed her in a no-nonsense tone. "This is where we pick up Maria. They'll bring her out in a wheelchair."

"A wheelchair? Is she okay?" She opened the passenger door.

"Well, she did break her arm, but I've brought Dad here before. The wheelchair is routine. You get her. I'll wait."

It took a while, but eventually, they were all back in the cab. Maria looked worn-out. "How are you feeling?" Carol asked tentatively.

"A bit tuckered out." Maria sighed. "But that might be the pain meds they gave me. At least I'm not in pain right now."

"Do you think you can do any grocery shopping?" Carol glanced at Victor. "We were going to stop and get a few things."

"I'll be fine." She patted Carol's arm with her good hand. "Now tell me, how did it go at the Grange?"

Carol briefly described what they'd accomplished as well as what she hoped to do next. "I guess the rest will have to wait until tomorrow. But at this rate, I'm sure it'll be done in time for the big night."

"That all sounds wonderful." Maria looked relieved. "Thank you so much."

They were able to complete their grocery shopping before poor Maria ran out of energy. Carol wasn't surprised to see her aunt dozing on the way home. Nobody spoke.

At the farmhouse, Victor helped Maria inside, but when

Carol invited him to stay a bit while she prepared a late lunch, he made excuses about needing to get his groceries home. Carol didn't buy it since his perishables would stay cold in the pickup. But she thought she understood his reasoning. His friendship with her had turned awkward at the dollar store—right after Victoria entered the picture. Well, there wasn't much she could do about that!

* * * *

The next morning, the day before the big Christmas Cotillion, Carol drove Maria's fully loaded car into town. Along with the bags from the dollar store, she had numerous lamps from Maria's house and some that Victor had dropped by on the porch late last night. She'd also put in a box of mason jars, a bag of tea lights, some carefully selected antiques, and even a portable CD player that Maria asked to bring to play Christmas music from. This time she even put in a neatly packed lunch that Maria insisted would be needed. She'd also insisted on coming along. Obviously curious about what her niece planned to do with all these miscellaneous items, or maybe just bored, Maria refused to take no for an answer but promised to remain on the sidelines while Carol finished the decorations.

"I really think I can wrap things up today," Carol said as she carefully drove down Maria's snow-packed driveway.

"Have you driven on snow before?" Maria asked.

"Not much."

"Well, the best advice I can give is to react slowly and smoothly. If the car should slide a bit, gently go with it and steer. No jerky moves. That can be disastrous."

"Right." Carol felt even more nervous now, and they weren't even on the real road.

"Have you ever been skiing?"

"Yes. I used to ski a lot in college. My roommate and her family were really into it."

"Well, think like you would if you were skiing. I never skied much myself, but that's what my Don used to tell new drivers. Relax, give yourself plenty of time, and make slow, smooth moves."

"Okay." Carol nodded. "That makes sense."

"Mind if I put on some Christmas music?"

Carol smiled. "Not at all."

"I have an old James Taylor CD in there now. It was Don's favorite." Maria turned on the audio, and Carol began to relax a bit more. With Christmas songs playing and Maria sweetly humming along, Carol was surprised at how quickly they got to town. And she wasn't even driving fast!

Carol unlocked the Grange door with a bit of trepidation. What if Maria didn't like what she'd done? Of course, she'd be fine to take it down and start over, but her feelings might be hurt. Reminding herself that professionals shouldn't allow their personal feelings or oversized egos to come before pleasing a client, she opened the door and let Maria go first, fumbling to flip on the lights that buzzed and flickered and finally began to illuminate the large space.

"Oh, my." Maria walked toward the center of the room, where tables were still set up with miscellaneous items strewn about.

Carol unzipped her parka. "Is it, uh, okay?"

"It's marvelous."

"Really?" Carol felt hopeful. "It's only half done."

"Well, I love it so far. I'm sure I'll love it more when you're finished."

Carol brought a folding chair over to her work area. "How about you sit here and you can supervise and direct."

"And stay out of your way?" Maria teased.

"I read the printed material urgent care sent home with you," Carol reminded her. "It said you need to take it easy. I'm just following instructions."

"Yes, yes, so you've told me already." Maria sighed and glanced around. "I'm surprised it's warm in here. Can you help me unzip this heavy coat?"

"I guess we forgot to turn the thermostat down." Carol helped Maria pull off the parka and ease herself into the chair. "Should I turn it down now?"

"No, leave it. We always run the furnace the day before the cotillion. Takes a day to take the chill off in here."

"Okay. I'm going to unload the car and then I'll get to decorating."

"Don't forget my little CD player. And grab that black case from the console while you're at it. It's got several good Christmas CDs."

With a background of cheerful Christmas music and her aunt's random comments and rambling narrative, Carol busily hung wreaths and garlands and ribbons until she could finally put her focus on the tables and create an ambiance that would feel warm and inviting.

"I noticed there's an abundance of tablecloths," Carol said, extracting several from a box she'd found the day before. She pulled out a Christmas calico, a solid red, and a cheery red-and-green plaid.

"Yes, over the years we've used different ones. Red one year, green the next, and so on. It's a way to appease all the women who've contributed them."

"Well, I thought it'd be interesting to use a combination of fabrics." Carol laid and lapped the three cloths over one table. "I'm going for sort of a country chic motif." She stepped back to look.

"Interesting." Maria drew out the word, as if she were a bit uncertain.

Now Carol arranged some of her dollar store items, along with some things from the storage room. Pausing to turn on the flickering battery lamp on the first table she'd set, Carol turned to Maria. "What do you think?"

Maria smiled. "I think it's lovely. Not like anything we've done before." She shook her head. "I suppose because we're all country bumpkins at heart, it never occurred to us to have a cotillion like that. Often the women have wanted glitz and glamour."

"I noticed there's plenty of sparkly decorations." Carol pulled out a few more tablecloths. "I hope you don't mind that I'm not using them. This old building seems uncomfortable with glitz. Kinda like a sweet old farm woman wearing a sequined gown and oversized rhinestones to a hoedown."

Maria laughed. "I happen to like country chic. And Gloria Davenport, bless her soul, isn't around to complain. Most of that glittery stuff was her contribution from back in the eighties."

Carol continued to work, experimenting with lighting and ways to keep the extension cords that she'd unearthed in the supply room from becoming trip hazards. She thought keeping the tables along the walls and securing things with a big roll of masking tape seemed to do the trick. It was work, but when she had all the lights going and turned off the hideous fluorescent lights, Maria let out a squeal of delight.

"Oh, Carol, it's just magical. I love it. Everyone is going to love it. How on earth did you even think of doing it like this?"

"To me light is key to good decor." Carol set the antique spinning wheel she'd borrowed from one of Maria's spare bedrooms on the long table she was arranging near the front entrance. "Without perfect lighting, a space never looks right." She continued to putter, setting out various pieces and doing her best to make the big room look inviting.

"Don't forget the refreshment table," Maria called out from her chair, pointing to a corner near the kitchen door. "It doesn't need much more than a tablecloth and a few greens or whatever."

"Hello?" a male voice called from the back of the room. "Anybody order a fireplace?"

"What?" Maria's eyes grew wide.

"Victor!" Carol exclaimed as he entered the space. "You remembered."

"Of course."

"Bring it up here." She waved to a spot she'd saved just in case the faux fireplace arrived. "I've got a braided rug and some things all set to go with it."

He set the stove in place, then looked around. "Wow, it looks almost like somebody's home in here."

"Yes!" Carol clapped her hands. "I wanted it to feel homey."

"Your country Christmas motif?" His tone was teasing, but he was smiling sweetly. "I really like it. Looks like you're almost finished . . ." He paused as the main front door swung widely open, letting in bright sunlight . . . and Victoria Snyder. Today she was dressed in a pale-blue parka trimmed in white fur. Her skinny jeans were neatly tucked into tall black boots, also trimmed with fur. And despite the fluffy white ski hat she wore, her blond hair looked impeccably styled, framing her face like she was ready for a photo op. With arms crossed in front of her, Victoria strolled the room, gazing about like she owned the joint.

"Well now, what do we have here?" She paused by a table. "Oh, I see, you've used your dollar store treasures. How quaint."

"It's country chic." Maria sounded as defensive as a mother hen. "Carol works for a fancy design firm in Seattle. She's a trained professional, and she felt this motif fit our old-fashioned Grange Hall. And I quite agree with her."

Victoria nodded. "Well, I'll admit it's a lot cozier in here with the low lighting—I always hated those awful fluorescent lights—but we all know how conservative some of the Grangers are about this hall and their cotillion." She laughed. "My daddy included. So it'll be interesting to see what they all have to say." She pointed at Victor. "You're the one I'm looking for. Apparently your phone is turned off or dead, as usual, but I've been trying to get ahold of you all day. If I hadn't seen your truck here, I probably would have driven out to your place, and you know what my Corvette is like on snow."

"A Corvette on snow." Maria shook her head. "That's just plain foolish."

"Well, my SUV has been in the shop for two weeks so it's all I have to get around town." She turned back to Victor, holding her hands out in exasperation. "You promised to call me since I couldn't get a clear answer from you yesterday."

Victoria looked at Maria, then pulled up a chair and sat next to her. "Can you believe this guy invited me to the cotillion and now seems to have completely forgotten all about it? And here I thought he had manners."

"That doesn't sound like Victor." Maria's gaze flickered to Carol.

Victor shifted uncomfortably. "I've been busy."

"I already got my dress." Victoria directed her attention to Maria. "You should see it. It's a strapless icy blue satin with this gorgeous crystal beadwork around the neckline. Fits me like a glove."

"Sounds chilly," Carol commented as she continued decorating.

"I have a stole," Victoria retorted. "And a handsome gentleman to keep me warm. That is, if he regains his memory."

"As I recall we talked about the cotillion some time ago." Victor cleared his throat. "In fact, if memory serves me, you were the one who brought it up quite casually, and I told you to get back to me on it. And when you didn't . . . well . . ." Victor shrugged. "I took it as a no-go."

Victoria stood before going over to him and looking straight into his eyes. "Oh, Victor, you know me. You've known me for years. I'm a procrastinator. But would I have gotten a new gown if I didn't plan to go with the handsomest guy in Miller's Creek?" She pouted. "I even got new shoes. Although I'm not sure how they'll do in this snow. I might need you to carry me in from the car." She laughed.

Suddenly Carol felt uncomfortable about her down-home decorations, more fitting for a hoedown than a fancy ball. "It, uh, sounds like the cotillion is a pretty formal affair . . ."

"It used to be," Maria said quickly.

"It *still* is," Victoria protested. "At least in the minds of *some* people. The more traditional ranch families, ones that have lived in Miller's Creek for generations."

"Oh, come now, I've seen it grow more casual with every passing year," Maria pointed out. "Some of the fellows just put on a clean shirt with blue jeans."

"That's what I'd do," Victor told them. "I mean, *if* I were coming."

"That's what I was afraid of." Victoria pouted again. "After I got my gorgeous gown, it would just figure you'd come as a cowboy." She tugged his arm. "Can we finish this conversation in private?"

He glanced around the room. "Guess I'm not needed here anyway."

"Come with me, Mr. Clarkson," she commanded. "I'll buy you a late lunch and a beer and we'll talk."

"Bye, ladies," he called in a flat, slightly helpless tone that Carol found particularly grating. Was he really that spineless? Or was he secretly relishing the attention from Victoria? Perhaps he even had feelings for that pushy woman. Maybe Carol would never know for sure. And maybe it didn't matter.

11

Finishing up the decorating took longer than Carol had anticipated. Probably because she became even more of a perfectionist after Miss Fashionista exited the Grange Hall. Not that she had any illusions she could please that snooty Victoria with the country chic motif. But hopefully Maria wouldn't get too much criticism for the way things looked tomorrow night.

"You were right about bringing our lunch today," Carol told Maria as she set the empty basket in the back seat. "I had no idea we'd be here all day. I hope it didn't wear you out."

"Sitting and listening to Christmas music and watching you transform the room?" Maria laughed from the passenger's seat. "I hardly think so."

"I was hoping we'd make it home before dark."

"Oh, we will," Maria assured her. "The sky is cloudless, and the snow is very reflective. Even as the sun is setting. Don't worry."

Carol closed the back door to the Grange, then paused to look around at the snow-covered town, where the light and shadows were painting everything in shades of pale blue. It really had been a beautiful day outside. Too bad she'd been cooped up in the Grange the whole time. But maybe she could get outside tomorrow. According to her phone, they had a few days of sunshine ahead. And she suspected, although it made no difference, that flights were now coming and going from Gerald R. Ford International Airport. As if to confirm this, she heard the low rumble of a jet overhead. Probably holiday travelers, off to see families. Well, she was with family now. As she slid into the driver's seat, she realized she wouldn't trade that for anything.

Still, she felt a nagging guilt about her mother's pleading the other night. But what was she supposed to do about it? Burden her aunt with her sister's accusations? Cave to her melodramatic mother? Neither option felt right. It was best to just let it be for now.

"I was just admiring how everything looks out here," she told her aunt as she started the car. "With the sun low in the sky, the light makes everything magical. Such a beautiful shade of pale blue."

"Kind of like Victoria and her gorgeous cotillion gown?" Maria said. "Pretty but ice cold."

Carol couldn't hold in her laugh.

"I can't help but think that girl was pigeonholing poor Victor today. And I think I know why."

Carol was all ears. "Pigeonholing?"

"Well, I suspect Victor might have mentioned the dance to her at one time. More likely she brought it up. It's hard to say, but I know Victor and if he made a commitment, even a slight one, he would keep it."

"Good for him." Carol nodded, focusing on the slick road.

"But I also know that girl. She has to get her way. She's a born competitor, and I'm sure she sees you as her competition."

"Competition?" Carol gaped at Maria, then instantly put her attention back on the road, gripping the wheel tightly. Focus, focus, focus.

"Sure. She can probably see it in Victor's eyes. He likes you and finds you attractive, and Victoria *cannot* stand it. Not so much because of Victor—I suspect she's not as interested in him as she puts on—but because that girl *cannot* stand to lose. She was homecoming queen, cheerleading queen, rodeo queen ... I probably missed a few titles, but my goodness, that girl collected enough crowns to start her own trophy shop. You have to give her credit though. She worked hard for them." Maria paused to catch her breath, then held up a forefinger. "And that girl worked hard to hook wealthy men too. And according to her, those divorces weren't failures. She claims she learned from them."

"Well, that's worth something." Carol wasn't sure she cared to know this much about Victoria.

"And what was worth more than that was the boatload of money she gained in the separations, which I'm sure made the partings sweet sorrows." Maria chuckled, then sobered. "But to be fair, Victoria's mother claims both marriages ended for very good reasons. I'm not surprised though. They sounded like bad matches from the start to me."

Carol didn't know what to say. Part of her felt sorry for Victoria and part of her thought she'd probably gotten what she deserved.

"Good grief, listen to me! I sound like a gossiping old hen." Maria let out a loud sigh. "Please forgive me. Do you think breaking my arm affected my head?"

Carol chuckled. "I don't think so. And I don't think of it as gossip as much as information. I appreciate knowing the rest of the story. Victoria has me more than a little bamboozled."

"And don't you pay any mind to her comments about the decor. That woman I mentioned earlier today, the one who liked all the glitz and glitter? Well, that was Gloria Davenport, and she was Victoria's aunt. They were, I'm certain, cut from the same cloth—and sequins must've been involved in the making."

Carol had to laugh. "It was weird because Victoria kinda reminded me of my mom today."

With those words, silence enveloped the car. The thick kind. Carol wondered if she shouldn't have mentioned her mom, although Maria had seemed okay about it before. Carol considered mentioning her late-night call but couldn't think of one good reason why.

"Carol." Maria paused for a long moment. "While you were loading my car this morning back at the house . . . well, I got a phone call." Her stilted voice had Carol's full attention.

"Uh-huh?" Carol, not wanting to be distracted from the slick roads, reminded herself about skiing, imagining a groomed slope . . . carefully gliding down.

"It was your mother."

"Oh?" Alarmed, Carol stole a quick glance at her aunt.

"I'm sorry. I don't want to upset you. Especially when you're driving."

"It's okay. I'm focusing on skiing." She attempted a laugh. "You can tell me what she said."

"No, no, I should wait until we get home."

"Really," Carol insisted, eyes fixed on the road. "I'll be dying of curiosity if you don't share, Aunt Maria. In fact, I'd been thinking about calling Mom back tonight. Did she mention that she called me the other night? Around midnight too." She shook her head. "I'm still processing that one."

"She didn't mention it."

Now the car got quiet and uncomfortable again. Did Maria have any idea what kind of allegations her sister had made against her?

"Well, Mom said some pretty harsh things," Carol confessed. Determined to get to the bottom of everything, she decided to be forthcoming. "It was a little disturbing, actually, and I've been hoping to clear the air with you."

"Yes, of course. By all means."

Now Carol spilled the beans, relaying her mom's mean accusations.

"Oh, wow." Maria exhaled loudly. "That's a lot to dump on you."

"I just want to know if any of it's true. I know my mom. She can be a real drama queen, and she's good at guilting people . . . or throwing big pity parties for herself. Believe me, I took her words with a grain of salt."

"Well, some of what she said is true. I did leave Rosa and Pop to get married. But good grief, I was twenty-seven then. And Rosa was almost seventeen. I thought it was about time she started taking care of herself. I'd done it for most of her life. And I hate to admit it, but I might've spoiled her. I guess I felt bad about her not having a mother."

"You didn't either."

"Yes. But she was so much younger. I tried to make up for it. I didn't even go to college, although I had a small scholarship to a school nearby." Maria sighed.

"Sounds like you really put your life on hold."

"I felt family should come first, but the truth is that Rosa started getting pretty rebellious as a teenager. She fought with me over everything. I honestly thought she'd be happier with me gone." Maria looked amused. "Well, until she figured out all the housework involved in caring for a home. I'd tried to break her in gradually, but expecting her to help out always started a big fight. I got tired of it."

"Who could blame you?"

"I blame myself some. If I'd been harder on her earlier on, maybe she would've learned to help out at a younger age. Although our father was always stepping in to protect her, saying she was too young for chores. He babied her even more than I did. But I always wondered if Rosa's life would've gone more smoothly if I'd done things differently."

"You were still a kid too," Carol argued. "How could you expect to know all that?"

"I suppose. But I always told myself I'd do it differently if I had kids. And that bit about our father being an alcoholic . . . well, I never saw him drink more than an occasional beer with a friend. As far as I was concerned, he was a good parent. If anyone is responsible for Rosa's less-than-desirable upbringing, it's me. I really didn't make a very good mother."

Carol didn't know what to say. Maria probably would've made a wonderful mother. Much better than the one Carol had endured during her own childhood.

"Anyway, I just thought you should know your mother is not very happy with either of us right now. She made that crystal clear with me."

"Yeah. Me too." She shared about Mom's displeasure with Carol putting the kibosh on the Bahamas. "But that was my choice and how she reacts to it is her problem." Still, Carol was surprised that her mom had called Maria. Hopefully she hadn't been too hard on her sister. "And by the way, I love being here with you in Michigan. I wouldn't trade the Bahamas for this."

"Really?" Maria sounded truly surprised.

"Absolutely. And just for the record, I think you'd have been a wonderful mom."

"And I think you must've been an ideal daughter—especially since you're a perfectly delightful niece."

Carol tightened her hands on the steering wheel. "I doubt my mother would agree with you on that."

"Rosa rarely agreed with me on anything."

"That's her misfortune."

"Well, I'll be keeping her in my prayers."

"Yeah." Carol nodded slowly. "Me too. At least, I'll try." She was relieved her aunt was so quick to forgive her sister, but she knew it was going to take her more time. Perhaps because she had more to forgive.

* * * *

After Carol finished cleaning up after dinner, Maria asked her to help in the bedroom. "I want to unearth something from my closet, but it's buried deep in the back, and I don't think I can get it with just one working arm."

"No problem." She followed Maria to her room. "What is it you're looking for?"

"An old dress . . ." Maria opened her closet door.

"Oh?"

"For the cotillion."

Carol studied Maria's bulky cast. Just helping her aunt into loose clothing was a bit of a challenge. Did she really expect to get into some fancy gown from days gone by?

"I thought you said people went for more casual apparel." Carol flipped on the closet light.

"Well, yes. We older folks choose comfort over style."

"That seems sensible." Carol surveyed the overflowing closet, wondering where to begin.

"I know, I know. My wardrobe needs a good thinning, but life always seems to get in the way. Goodness, I must have forty years' worth of clothes stuffed in here. Antonia thinks I should sell some of these old things on some vintage website, but honestly, besides not being that clever with technology, I have just never found the time."

"So . . . do you have any idea where this old dress might be?"

"Oh, yes. It's down on that end." She pointed to the right. "Behind a lot of decrepit coats that are probably vintage too. It's a burgundy color. Probably near the wall. I always keep it alongside my wedding dress, and that's in a black garment bag."

"Okay." Carol struggled to push the hangers of clothes to one side, making room to thumb through the remaining hangers. "Since you store it with your wedding dress, I'm guessing it's pretty special. But do you really think you can get into it? I mean, with your arm and all."

"Mercy no!" Maria laughed. "It's not for me, Carol."

She paused and looked at her aunt. "Oh?"

"I, uh, I thought you might want to borrow it."

Carol cringed inwardly at the idea of wearing her aunt's musty old cotillion dress. She could only imagine what it might look like. But, of course, she didn't want to hurt Maria's feelings.

"The fabric is a mix of lace and velvet and satin ribbon trim. It was a Gunne Sax dress. You probably never heard of that brand. They were quite the thing back in the seventies. I was in my twenties when I bought my first one. Back then it was pretty spendy for me, but I loved that dress dearly. I wore it on a few dates with Don and even years later, when he took me to our first cotillion."

Carol spotted something burgundy and tugged it out. She was surprised to see a fairly attractive dress in a Boho-chic style. Like Maria had said, it was a combination of burgundy lace, velvet, and satin ribbon. She held it out so they could both examine it. The tea-length dress had a high waist and full skirt.

Maria eagerly reached for the hanger, taking it with her as she sat down in the nearby chair. "Oh, the good times I had in this dress."

"It's very pretty. And seems to have held up okay." Carol slid her phone from her back pocket and began a quick search. A lot of Gunne Sax dresses immediately popped up on several websites. And they were not cheap.

"Might need a needle and thread here or there . . . and could use a good airing out and steaming . . ." Maria mused. "But some people thought it was rather striking back in the day."

Still online, Carol found a dress that resembled her aunt's and blinked at the high price.

"It was such fun to wear it back when I was young . . . with my long dark hair." Maria looked wistfully up at Carol. "In fact, my hair was a lot like yours." She smiled. "Anyway, I've heard some young women like these vintage dresses."

"No doubt about that." Carol held her phone out so Maria could see the online listing that priced dresses like this one just under a thousand dollars. "Look what you could get for it."

"Oh, my. That's crazy!" Maria firmly shook her head. "But I could never sell it."

"No, no, of course not."

"Do you think . . . well, I wouldn't want to push it on you . . . but if you'd like to wear it for the cotillion, I'd be honored." She held the dress out to Carol.

"Really?" She took the dress from her aunt. "Do you think it'd even fit? That bodice looks small." She held it up to her, standing in front of the full-length mirror on the closet door. It really was pretty.

"One way to find out."

"I think I should take a shower first," Carol told her. "I feel kind of grubby after decorating all day."

"Yes. You go do that. Then we'll have a little fashion show."

It didn't take long to clean up, but by the time Carol came back down wearing a borrowed bathrobe, Maria already had a steamer out and was awkwardly attempting to steam the dress.

"Let me do that." Carol reached for the small appliance.

"So many tasks I took for granted when I had two good arms."

"Fortunately your condition is just temporary." Carol steamed the skirt, fluffing it out as she did. "My boss's husband had a stroke and permanently lost use of his right arm. That was hard."

Maria started sharing about various times she'd worn the dress, including the night she got engaged.

Carol wiped a tear from her eye. "No wonder it's special." The dress was finished now and looking even better than before.

"Go try it on in there," Maria pointed to the master bath. "I can't wait to see if it fits."

It didn't take long to slip it on and pull the zipper up. She could only see the top half of the dress in the sink mirror, but the fitted bodice seemed about perfect and the sweetheart neckline was surprisingly becoming.

She stepped out to show Maria. "I've never worn anything like this. But it seems to fit, and it's comfortable."

Maria's dark eyes grew wide as she led Carol back to the full-length mirror. "Oh, my goodness, Carol. You look beautiful."

Carol stared at her image, then smiled. "It really does look good, doesn't it?"

"It's absolutely perfect."

Carol did a little spin, watching the skirt flow out. "It would be good for dancing." Her smile vanished. "But it's so valuable. I don't think I should wear—"

"Nonsense. How can a dress be valuable if it spends all its time in the back of a closet. No, this dress wants to go to the cotillion. It wants to dance again."

Carol considered this, then frowned. "But don't I need a date to go to the cotillion?"

"I don't have a date and I'm going." Maria sighed, reminding Carol this would be her aunt's first year without her husband. "You can be my date, and we'll sit with Antonia and Larry. Antonia will appreciate the company since Larry's verbal skills are so limited and folks don't visit with him as much anymore. His mobility issues keep him off the dance floor too. This might be his last year at the cotillion, so please don't let lack of a date give you cold feet."

"I would like to see the event," Carol confessed. "Just to see how the decorations look at night." She hated to admit she was equally curious as to how the guests would react. What if they hated what she'd done? In that case, she might be better

off at home. "I don't know though," she said. "Being dateless
. . . maybe I'll take a pass, after all."

"Well, I can't drive myself there and I fully intend to go. If
you won't be my date, I suppose I'll have to stay home too. But
I would hate to miss it."

Carol felt guilty now. How could she be so selfish? "Okay,
I'll be your date. But I'd be more comfortable dressed casually.
I think this beautiful dress is too much for—"

"It is not too much!" Maria argued. "You heard Victoria
bragging about her fancy gown. Good grief, she'll be decked
out like prom night. And like I said, young folks tend to dress
up more than us oldies."

Carol poked out a bare toe. "But I don't know what shoes
I'd wear. My sandals for the Bahamas sure won't work in the
snow."

"I always wore my dress boots with it at the cotillion. A pair
of knee-high black leather ones, but of course, I don't have
those anymore. All I have these days are cowgirl boots or snow
boots." She chuckled.

"Cowgirl boots?" Carol glanced at the closet.

"Sure. I've got several pairs. But would you really want those
with that dress?"

"Cowgirl boots with dresses are still a thing. Mind if I poke
around?"

Maria waved her forward with her good arm. "You know
I don't."

Carol poked around until she found a handsome dark brown
pair. She slipped them onto her bare feet, then came back to
check the combo in the mirror. "Not bad." She smiled. "Not
bad at all."

"I have to admit, I like it." Maria smiled as well.

Carol hugged her aunt. "I feel like Cinderella going to the
ball."

"I don't mind playing fairy godmother." Maria laughed,

then grew somber. "I actually offered to be your godmother when you were first born, but your mother wouldn't have it."

"Too bad." Carol wondered how much different her life might've gone if Maria had been in the picture while she was growing up. Of course, this only reminded her of Mom and she preferred not to think about her right now.

"Well, I'm glad we got tomorrow night all settled." Maria yawned.

"Yes, but it's late. We should be getting you to bed." Carol carefully removed the dress and hung it up, then she helped her aunt prepare for bed, finally tucking her in and kissing her good night. Then she quietly picked up the dress and boots and rather reverently carried them up to her room so she could hang the dress on a peg by the closet door. For a long moment, she stood just staring at the vintage dress, imagining what it would feel like to be Victor's date tomorrow night . . . then reminding herself that would be Victoria's pleasure. And, really, if that's the kind of woman Victor wanted, he could have her. After all, didn't their names say it all? Victoria the victorious . . . wanting to win Victor. Well, let her!

Shooing these troublesome thoughts away, she distracted herself by getting ready for bed, but before turning off the light, she silenced her phone. Just in case her mom decided to give her another late-night call.

Although she felt a smidgen of guilt, she just couldn't deal with any more mama drama tonight, especially after discovering her mother had twisted the story, pretending she'd been a small child when Maria had left. It was obviously just another pathetic attempt to turn Carol away from her aunt. It was one thing to want a mother-daughter rendezvous in the Bahamas but throwing Maria under the bus like that felt unforgivable. And yet she knew she needed to follow her aunt's lead, like she'd said she would, and forgive her mom. At the same time, she rationalized that the wounds she bore from her mother ran deeper than Maria's. For that reason alone, it should naturally take longer.

But since she had promised Maria she would pray for Mom, she did her best. And the best she could muster, like she'd done for other "enemies" in the past, was to ask God to bless her mom. She'd once heard a sermon about how asking God to bless someone didn't necessarily mean they'd win the lottery or become a celebrity . . . because sometimes God's best blessing came in the form of a good spanking. In the case of her mom, she hoped for the latter!

12

After the past few days of decorating and caring for her aunt, Carol was grateful for a peaceful day at the farmhouse. With snow all around outside, Christmas decorations strewn about, and a glowing fire inside, it was the perfect setting for relaxation. Except a certain something was niggling in her mind until she finally had to give in to it. *Just get it over with*, she told herself. She would call her mom.

For starters, she planned to question Mom about the false accusations she'd made against Maria. She hoped to do it in a controlled and nonconfrontational way, but she knew it would be a challenge. Although it might be easier if she initiated the conversation instead of waiting for her mom to call and catch her off guard again. So, while Maria was napping in the early afternoon, Carol slipped upstairs and called her mom.

The phone rang so many times, she wondered if perhaps her mother really had disowned her. And if so, there was not much she could do about that. She was about to hang up when her mom's groggy voice muttered "Hello."

"Oh, you are there." Carol tried to corral her thoughts again. "So you're still talking to me, after all."

Her mom just grunted.

"Did I wake you?"

"Not exactly. I was about to get up."

Carol knew it was past noon in Arizona but had the wisdom not to mention it. "Well, I talked to Maria about the things you told me, and it seems there's another side to the story."

"Are you calling me a liar?"

"No, but I know enough about memories to know that people can experience the same situation and remember it completely differently."

"Yeah, I've heard about that."

"Anyway, Maria explained that you were, uh, actually a teenager when she married Don."

"I never said I wasn't."

"I thought you said you were a small child."

"Well, if that's what you think you heard, maybe it's your memory that's wacky."

Carol bristled but held her tongue.

"All I know is that Maria was very selfish," Mom continued. "She left me high and dry, and I had to fend for myself. It was very hard. Very traumatic."

"Maria was twenty-seven, Mom. She'd taken care of you for most of her life. It was time for her to live her own life."

"What about *my* life? Being left alone?"

"You were almost seventeen. When I was that age, you used to leave me home alone with no parent in the house, sometimes for days at a time. In fact, I think I was even younger when you decided I didn't need a full-time parent around."

There was a brief pause. "You were very mature for your age."

"Thank you, but maybe I didn't feel mature."

"Did you call just to make me feel guilty, Carol? I already have a splitting headache and do not need your—"

"I'm sorry. That's not why I called. Mostly I wanted to clear things up with you after Maria told me her side of the story. And just for the record, she was very gracious toward you. In fact, she even blames herself for how you grew up."

"Well, she should! Not that I believe her. She probably just said that."

"I believe her. She really wishes she'd done things differently." Carol refrained from saying how she wished she'd been tougher on her baby sister.

"Hmm, if that's true, I guess it's reassuring . . . Not that it changes anything."

"Well, that's between you and her. I only called to say that I don't like you trying to turn me against Maria. She's my aunt and I love her. But I love you too, Mom." She had to control herself from adding, "Even when you're acting like a selfish egotistical narcissist."

"Humph. Well, I suppose that's worth something."

Carol waited for the next barb.

"And for what it's worth, I love you too, Carol. And I'm not disowning you as my daughter." She laughed. "Don't worry, I haven't taken you out of my will . . . yet."

Carol forced a feeble laugh.

"Have you changed your mind about the Bahamas? I got to thinking last night that it's not too late. We could just stay longer and—"

"No thanks. To be honest, the Bahamas don't even interest me now." She stood to gaze out her window. "You should see it here, Mom. It's so beautiful. Snow everywhere, blue sky, fresh air. And Maria's farmhouse is charming. So peaceful and restful. We're going to an old-fashioned Christmas dance tonight. And we'll have neighbors and friends here for Christmas Eve dinner. Italian food too. I wish you could come, Mom. I think you'd enjoy it."

There was such a long silence on the other end, Carol wondered if her mom had hung up. But perhaps she was more worried that her mom was actually considering coming. Despite the invitation, Carol wasn't sure having her cantankerous mother here would be too nice for anyone.

"Well, you paint a pretty picture, darling, but I'll pass. At least for this year. Maybe someday. You never know."

"Maybe you and I will take a vacation together someday," Carol added with forced enthusiasm. She couldn't actually imagine how complicated a trip like that could get. Most likely it would never happen anyway.

"Well, I hope you and Maria have a good Christmas together." Mom's tone sounded flat again. "And in case you're interested, your stepfather has been a bit nicer to me lately. Apparently, he didn't really want me to fly the coop after all." She laughed, but it sounded hollow.

"Thanks. You have a good Christmas too." Carol swallowed hard, surprised that she suddenly felt tearful. "You and Ed are in my prayers."

Mom cleared her throat. "Well, I guess that's a good thing. I suppose we heathens need it." Again, a hollow laugh.

"I love you, Mom."

"I love you too, Carol Louise."

After they hung up, Carol really did cry. Not long and hard and painful. Just a good cleansing sort of cry. She knew she'd forgiven her mother, and there was a certain release and freedom that came with that. But it was also bittersweet—the realization that Mom was Mom and she always would be. Carol might as well beat her head against a wall as expect her mother to change.

Finally, she washed her face with cold water and, thinking they might have a long night ahead with the cotillion, took a nap.

When she woke up, the sky was already dusky, but according to her phone, it was barely four. The plan for tonight, according to Maria, was to have a light dinner, then get dressed before heading out to the Grange, where they would arrive early enough to make sure everything looked just right before the big night.

After cleaning up the dinner things and helping Maria to

select her own outfit for the evening—a dark green silk blouse and sleek black pants—Carol went upstairs to dress. It was a rather simple affair. Just the dress, a borrowed slip, and the boots with a pair of warm socks underneath. But when she saw her hair hanging limply over her shoulders, she decided to do something. After pinning it up in a loose bun with a few soft tendrils hanging down, she applied a bit of makeup. Not too much, just a little color for her lips and cheeks and a touch of eye shadow. She had packed minimal jewelry for the Bahamas, but eventually settled for her favorite silver hoops. Plain but pretty.

She went downstairs to find Maria partially dressed and fumbling to open a jewelry box. "Can I help you?" Carol offered.

"Yes. This latch is stubborn. Like me." Maria chuckled. "I wanted something in there for tonight."

"How about I help you finish dressing first?" Carol suggested.

"Yes. Managing buttons and zippers is a challenge."

"There." Carol finished the last blouse button, then picked up the jewelry box. "What are you looking for?"

"For starters, my squash blossom pendant and some earrings I like to wear with this blouse." She reached in for the pieces and waited as Carol helped her put them on.

"You look very pretty," Carol told her.

"For an old lady, anyway. But thank you." Maria crossed to the closet door mirror to inspect herself. "And there's another old necklace in that box. You might have to dig a little. It's nothing too elaborate or expensive. Don got it for me on our first Christmas. It's a silver chain with garnet drops, and it went nicely with the Gunne Sax dress."

Carol extracted and untangled a chain that seemed to fit the description. "It's pretty."

"Needs a bit of polishing." Maria pointed to a small flannel square. "Give it a rub then."

Carol polished the silver chain until it shone, then took it over to the mirror and put it on. "It does go nicely, but it's special. I don't think I should wear it tonight. What if I broke it or lost it?"

Maria waved her good hand. "Never mind about that. Like I said with the dress, I'd rather have these things go to good use than be hidden away forever." She suddenly blinked as if seeing Carol for the first time. "Oh, my dear girl. You do look lovely."

"Thanks to my fairy godmother."

"You'll be the belle of the ball tonight."

"More like a wallflower."

"Trust me, you look nothing like a wallflower." She pointed to the alarm clock by her bed. "Now, if we want to be there in time to check on everything, we need to get moving pronto."

* * * *

It didn't take as long as Maria had anticipated to have the Grange Hall all set for the evening. And with softer lamps and electric lanterns glowing, it looked even better in the nighttime than in the day. But Carol didn't mind having spare time because it was interesting to help the chattering Grange women fussing about in the kitchen. At first Carol assumed they were stereotypical "farm wives" who possibly lived in the shadows of their traditional farmer spouses, but after helping the loquacious ladies set up the food and drinks, she was surprised to discover that the woman in charge, Maggie Pierson, was a divorcee who'd inherited a large cattle ranch that she'd been managing on her own for several decades now. And Lucille Vaughn, a quiet, industrious widow with short gray hair, managed her own two hundred acres with the help of several farmhands.

Realizing that trying to help in the kitchen was wearing Maria out, Carol suggested they go sit down at a table in the main hall. As they exited the kitchen, an older couple was just coming in the main door.

"There's Antonia and Larry," Maria told Carol. "Victor's mama and pop." She called out to the couple, waiting for their

128

slow approach since Larry was moving awkwardly with the help of a cane. After introductions, Maria led the way to a table along the wall.

"I'm so happy to finally meet you," Antonia told Carol after they all sat down. She turned to her husband. "This is that gal Victor told us about, Larry." She said Carol's name slowly. "Carol."

His eyes lit up. "*Christmas* Carol?"

Carol laughed. "As a matter of fact, yes."

Of course, Maria used this opportunity to explain about Carol's birthday being on Christmas. After the normal reactions that she usually tried to avoid by keeping her birthdate under wraps, she confessed that she usually wasn't one to celebrate.

"It's always been sort of awkward," she said. "People either feel sorry for you or they act like it's something special."

"It *is* something special." Antonia patted her hand. "You share your special day with our Lord and Savior. What a privilege for you."

"I guess so." Carol didn't know what to say, suddenly feeling guilty for all the times she'd complained about her birthday.

"Christmas Carol," Larry said again. "You sing?"

Carol laughed. "Not so well. But I do enjoy it."

"Good." He nodded. "Pretty girl. Sing pretty."

"Not right now, Larry," Antonia quietly said.

"We'll all sing carols on Christmas Eve," Maria assured him. "With all our friends and neighbors. Just like we always do."

He nodded with a slightly vacant expression.

"And what about Carol's birthday?" Antonia asked Maria. "I'd like to do something special to celebrate with her on Christmas Day."

"No, no, that's okay," Carol said quickly. Besides not wanting any special attention, the idea of Victor's mother planning something for her felt awkward. "We'll just have had a busy evening on Christmas Eve. I don't want you to go to any trouble for—"

"No trouble. In fact, Victor and I will cook something really special for you," Antonia told Maria.

"You'll get no complaints from me," Maria said.

"A party for Carol," Antonia told Larry.

"Pretty Carol," he said pleasantly. "Good for her."

"She is pretty, isn't she?" Antonia said before turning back to Carol. "And I think I recognize your dress. Isn't it Maria's?"

Maria confirmed this and the women began making favorable comments on Carol's appearance, almost as if she weren't there.

Finally, feeling uncomfortable, she stood. "I, uh, I'm thirsty. Can I get you folks something to drink? They have a tasty cranberry punch and some hot tea. And I'll bet the coffee is ready to serve by now." She took their orders and, eager to escape, excused herself. She didn't mind that they approved of her appearance, but she didn't want to just sit and listen. And besides that, she needed to figure out a way to put the brakes on their birthday plans for her. Partly because it was embarrassing, but mostly because the idea of being in Victor's home just felt plain awkward. Yet she didn't want to appear ungrateful or put a damper on their festive evening tonight. As she walked to the kitchen, she decided to ask Maria to help her sort it all out tomorrow.

When she emerged with a tray of drinks, a three-piece band was just setting up on the little stage. She paused from navigating the throng of guests streaming in to check them out. A young woman wearing a flowing floral skirt was tuning a violin while a bearded man plucked a few notes on his guitar and another removed a mandolin from a case.

Several female guests milled about the bandstand, visiting among themselves and pointing about the room. She didn't like to eavesdrop but couldn't help herself.

"Doesn't this look inviting?" a redheaded woman said. "And wasn't that nice to have a stove to warm up at by the entrance?" "Maria really outdid herself this year." A younger woman pointed to a nearby table. "Don't you love those little lanterns?" "Yes, but I don't know how Maria managed all this," a third woman said. "I heard she was laid up with a broken arm." "Yes, but Margie Kincaid told me her niece helped her," the redhead said.

Just as the band began to play a bluegrass version of "Jingle Bells," three men joined the women, and all of them chatted away like it was a happy reunion. Feeling encouraged by the women's comments, Carol brought her tray back to the table where her older companions were still waiting. So maybe she'd been worried about nothing. Victoria's criticism had probably just been an attempt to put Carol in her place—to remind her she was the outsider.

Carol smiled pleasantly as she served the drinks, then sat down with her own coffee. But as she observed more couples streaming in, cheerfully greeting each other as they removed winter coats—hugging, patting backs, obviously at home here in the Grange—she began to feel out of place again. There was no denying she truly was the outsider here. Not only was she from "another world," she didn't even have a date. Maria and Antonia were chattering about an upcoming quilt show, and Larry was staring blankly at the crowd, possibly feeling as much on the outside as she. Although Maria had mentioned that Larry had been the Grange president for years before his illness worsened. Carol felt a nudge at her elbow and turned to see Antonia looking at her.

"Tell me about yourself," Antonia said. "About all I know is you're an interior decorator from Seattle."

Carol considered this. There didn't seem to be much to say beyond that at the moment, but she decided to try. Digging deeper, she shared about an interest in gardening. "Unfortunately, I live in a condo so I have to make do with container gardening on my terrace, but I've had good success with tomatoes and cucumbers and herbs and flowers . . . and it really makes my terrace pretty and green all summer."

"Plants must grow well in Seattle's wet, mild climate."

"Yes. It makes me wish for a bit more room to grow. Occasionally I play with the idea of finding property with enough land and maybe some greenhouses. And then I'd grow lots of flowers and maybe even start a small floral design business."

"Oh, that sounds like fun."

"Yes. But land is pretty spendy in my area."

"That could be challenging."

"I guess I need more affordable dreams." She shrugged, trying to think of any other interests she could tell her about. "I've often wished I'd taken more time to learn how to cook."

Antonia's brows arched. "You don't know how to cook?"

Carol shook her head glumly. "Cooking or any kind of homemaking never interested my mother, so I never really learned. Most of the time I'm content with microwave meals, but sometimes I wish I had skills like yours."

"Don't we all," Maria chimed in. "No one cooks like Antonia. Well, except Victor. He's got the gift too."

Antonia looked proud. "Victor is far more accomplished than I am."

"Well, I admire you both," Carol confessed. "I doubt I could ever learn to cook something like lasagna. Even if I did, I doubt anyone would want to eat it. By the way, your lasagna was amazing."

Antonia waved a dismissive hand. "Learning to cook is easy. Like rolling off a log."

"My attempts at fancy cuisine usually tasted like they'd rolled off a log." Maria laughed. "Lucky for me, Don and I always liked simple food."

As Antonia and Maria continued to compare cooking fiascos and triumphs, Carol noticed that the room had filled with guests and a few couples were already dancing to the peppy music. Realizing how left out Larry seemed, she turned to him. "Did you used to like to dance?"

His eyes opened wide, and he nodded eagerly. "Yes. I dance." Using the table to balance himself, he started to push himself up from the chair.

"Oh, Larry." Antonia rested a hand on his arm. "I don't think—"

"Yes." He nodded at Carol. "Dance!"

Carol didn't know what to do. She hadn't meant to invite him to dance, but he seemed to think that was her intent. "Is it okay?" she quietly asked Antonia.

She chuckled. "Well, it's up to you, sweetie. I'm not sure he'll last out there for more than a few steps, but go ahead and give it a try. He'll probably wear you out just leaning on your arm."

Larry was already on his feet and reaching for his cane.

Carol linked her arm under his. "Maybe you should leave your cane behind. You can lean on me while we dance," she told him, hoping that would work.

Antonia nodded her affirmation as she took her husband's cane, and Carol slowly, very slowly, led Larry to the dance floor, where, to her relief, he managed to move a bit more gracefully than she expected. It wasn't exactly a dance, but it was close, and he seemed to be enjoying himself. Even though she was grateful for her height and strength, and that she was able to offer him some support and keep him balanced, she was still relieved when the song ended with Larry on his feet.

"That was great," she told him. "How about we have a rest and try it again later?"

He nodded. "Later. Yes."

She looped her arm through Larry's again, and they slowly, very slowly, retreated to rejoin Antonia and Maria. About half-way there, Carol noticed an attractive blond near the main entrance. Looking like a celebrity, the woman removed a fur-trimmed white cape to reveal a sparkling, pale-blue gown. Carol realized it was Victoria . . . with Victor. She looked like the cotillion queen, and at her side, Victor was neatly dressed in black jeans, a white shirt and dark plaid vest, and a black bolo tie. Country debonair. Victoria linked arms with him as several well-dressed friends boisterously greeted them. The whole group, compared to her table, seemed full of youth and holiday cheer, obviously ready for a good time. Carol suddenly realized Larry was weaving ever-so-slightly. Worried he was tired, she diverted her attention from the striking couple and their noisy friends in order to navigate her slightly impaired and somewhat elderly partner back to the safety of the table, where Antonia and Maria both watched with wide eyes.

"Larry is a fabulous dancer," she told the women as she and Antonia helped ease him into a chair.

"I had no idea you could still dance." Antonia kissed her husband's cheek, then shook her head in disbelief. "That was wonderful," she whispered to Carol. "Thank you for asking him."

Carol didn't want to correct the misconception that she'd asked Larry to dance. After all, it had turned into a happy mistake. "If Larry wants to try it again after a rest, I'd love to be his partner." She lowered her voice. "Well, unless you want to dance with—"

"No thank you," Antonia said emphatically. "The last time we attempted to dance turned disastrous." Her smile turned sad. "So I'll warn you, dear, do so at your own risk."

"Right." Carol nodded, imagining the sweet old guy splayed across the floor with a room of onlookers gawking while she tried to get him to his feet. Maybe one dance was enough.

C arol moved the angle of her folding chair to focus on the people at her table instead of the dance floor. She had no intention of gaping at Victor and Victoria as they worked the room. They were obviously in their element and confident about their place in this crowd. They were probably preparing to dance the night away. More than ever she felt like an outsider, a misfit, and a wallflower. If there was any way to gracefully slip out, she would gladly do so. But how? Claim a headache? Call a taxi to take her home? But then Maria would be stuck with the car. Perhaps Antonia and Larry could give her a ride. The idea was tempting.

She turned to Maria and Antonia, who were engrossed in a conversation about their Christmas Eve plans. And so Carol just excused herself to the little girls' room, where she entered a stall and pulled out her phone. Not that she had anyone to call. She briefly entertained the idea that a taxi could take her to the airport. But besides it being unlikely any taxi would take her the whole way to Grand Rapids, she knew that would be a selfish plan, not to mention impossible to explain to her aunt. How could she abandon Maria like that? And simply because she was having a bad evening. *Grow up*, she told herself, reaching to unlatch the stall door. She paused at the sound of voices.

"Oh, Victoria," a woman said lightly, "you're too modest. We all agree that your gown is absolutely gorgeous. Perfection."

"She's just fishing for compliments," another woman said a bit wryly.

"Maybe it's because Victor didn't even mention my dress when he picked me up." Victoria sounded truly wounded.

"Well, seriously, Vicki," a high-pitched voice retorted, "if there was a cotillion queen, the crown would go to you, so get over it."

"Besides, you know men," the first one added. "They're always slow on the uptake when it comes to fashion."

"Maybe so," High Voice said, "but Victor sure looks nice tonight."

"So stop fretting over it," another said. "Count your blessings."

The sound of running water muffled Victoria's response.

"Yeah, he's quite the catch," High Voice said. "Just be thankful, girlfriend."

"But he was so chilly to me tonight. And when I invited him in for drinks when he picked me up, he flat-out refused and said we had to go."

"You're overblowing this whole thing," High Voice said. "Victor seems perfectly happy to be here with you. Just enjoy it."

A flushing toilet drowned out Victoria's response again.

"Cheer up," one of them said. "I'll bet he was just nervous." Victoria huffed. "What does he have to be nervous about?"

"Jason told me he's getting ready to pop the question," High Voice said.

"Seriously?" Victoria's tone brightened. "Jason said that?"

"Yep. And he's Victor's best friend. He should know."

"I sure hope third time's the charm for you," High Voice said with an exasperated tone. "I draw the line at being maid of honor more than three times."

The others all laughed.

"I can't believe you're in here having a pity party. Good grief, girl, looks like you'll get a diamond for Christmas." More exasperation.

All the women took turns razzing and congratulating their "poor" friend. And finally, to Carol's relief, the noisy flock exited the bathroom.

Feeling guilty for eavesdropping, yet trying to process what she'd just overheard, Carol emerged from the stall and washed her hands. Then, as a pair of older women came in bickering about the number of calories in storebought eggnog, she quietly slipped out.

Larry's eyes lit up when Carol returned to the table. "Dance?" he asked. Unsure how to respond, she looked to Antonia, who just shrugged, and then to her aunt, who was chuckling.

"Why not?" Maria asked.

"Okay." Carol smiled at Larry, who was already struggling to stand. With the help of his wife and Carol, he was soon on his feet and taking Carol's hand, shuffling out to the dance floor, where a rather lively tune was playing. Uncertain Larry could keep up with the beat, she decided to just follow his lead. But to her surprise, he began moving a bit more limberly out there. Holding on to her—partly for support, she felt certain—he continued to shuffle her out to the center of the floor, grinning the whole while.

She didn't even flinch each time he stepped on her toes, but when he started weaving to one side, she worried about his balance and held him a bit tighter. She glanced back at the table, which suddenly seemed about a mile away, then tried to direct him back in that direction, but he was leaning even more now, precariously close to falling. She tried not to imagine the humiliation if they both tumbled to the floor. And, she worried, what if he got hurt?

She was about to stop the dance and beg someone for help when she felt a hand on her shoulder and turned to see Victor putting a firm arm around his dad's waist. "Can I break in?" he asked with a big grin.

"Yes," she gasped in relief. "I think we could use a hand."

"Dance?" Larry smiled at his son.

"Yes." Victor nodded, still holding on to his dad. "Let's all dance."

"Yes." Larry nodded eagerly. "Dance." He didn't seem to mind the help but was still clinging tightly to Carol.

Somehow, to Carol's enormous relief, Victor managed to dance the three of them back to the table and, after peeling his dad's hands off of Carol, got the old guy seated. Both Antonia and Maria looked shocked but were soon giggling over what must've been quite a spectacle.

"I'm sorry," Antonia whispered to Carol. "I should've said no, but Larry was so happy and having such a good time."

"We did have fun." Carol patted Larry's hand. "Thank you for the dance. I will remember it always."

He nodded as if he understood, but his expression was vague. Antonia put an arm around him. "You probably wore yourself out cutting the rug like that out there, Larry." She pushed a cup toward him. "Have some punch."

Victor turned to Carol now. "How about finishing that dance with me?" he asked. "Unless my dad objects."

"Go," his mother whispered to him. "Poor Carol deserves a good dance after that."

So Victor took her hand and led her back out. Another lively song was playing, but to her pleasure, Victor was a good dancer. And she suddenly was grateful for the cowboy swing lessons she'd taken in her twenties. Before long, they were swinging and spinning, and it was pure fun. The song ended with a twirl that wound her into his arms, nearly knocking him off-balance.

"Taking after your dad?" she teased, and they both burst out laughing.

"Hey, he used to be quite a dancer," Victor told her. "Taught me everything I know."

"He's such a sweet guy. I can imagine that." She glanced around, suddenly feeling self-conscious. "And thanks for the dance, but I have a feeling your, uh, Victoria will be wanting to dance—"

"Vicki isn't much into dancing tonight," he told her. "I guess her fancy dress makes it difficult. So no worries." The next song was starting, another peppy one, and he reached for her hand. "Go again?"

She shrugged. "Why not?"

So, for the second time, they swung and twirled, and every move he initiated, she finished, as if it had been choreographed. She couldn't remember ever having this much fun on the dance floor. When the next song began, he was still holding her hand, insisting on "one more." But this one was a slow dance. Still, he didn't miss a beat as he took her in his arms, holding her close. As they moved gracefully together, she felt herself melting . . . and falling . . . not on the ground . . . in love perhaps? No, of course not, she chided herself as she spotted Victoria nearby. The thought was ridiculous. Victoria was dancing with one of her friends, but she didn't seem to be enjoying herself. Instead, she was staring daggers at Carol and Victor. But Carol just looked the other way.

When the song ended, Carol told Victor she needed a break. She felt quite flushed and warm but not from the dancing. She knew she could dance all night with him without complaining. Well, unless Victoria killed her. "I need something cool to drink," she said.

"Me too." He led her to the refreshment table where they got drinks and donuts and then he escorted her back to Maria and his parents, pulling out her chair before sitting down with them. As Victor made congenial conversation, Carol glanced toward Victoria, who was now standing with her girlfriends and definitely simmering. Carol was tempted to remind Victor about his date but wasn't quite sure how. After all, he was a grown man. If he wasn't worried, why should she be?

"You two danced beautifully," Antonia told them.

"Yes," Maria agreed, "you should go out there again. It was a pleasure to watch you." She pointed to Carol. "I knew Victor was an exceptional dancer, but I had no idea you were so talented."

Carol confessed to having had lessons. "But it was ages ago. I didn't even know that I remembered."

"Well, you were a natural," Antonia said.

"I always thought that was a good dancing dress," Maria told her.

"And very pretty too," Victor added with a twinkle in his eyes. "Want to go again?"

"Let me finish my punch," she said. Then seeing a flash of pale blue moving toward her, she set down her drink and braced herself.

"Victor," Victoria said primly. "I've been looking all over for you. I thought maybe you'd gone home."

Carol bit her tongue, controlling herself from calling Victoria's bluff. She'd just observed Victoria glaring at them.

"Just visiting with my folks here," he told her casually. "Care to join us?"

"No, thank you." She folded her arms in front of her. "Would you care to join me with my friends?"

He held up his drink and half-eaten donut. "Mind if I finish this first? I didn't have dinner tonight and I'm—"

"You didn't eat?" She arched her fair brows. "I offered you drinks and appetizers at my house, but you claimed you weren't hungry and—"

"I wasn't hungry at the time. But dancing must've—"

"You weren't dancing with me." She sounded indignant.

He stood now, facing her. "You said you didn't care to dance."

"Does that give you the right to run off and leave me like that? To dance with another girl? Don't you think that's very impolite?"

"Hey, it's a dance, Vicki." He held out his hands. "We always dance with other people. There are no rules about that."

"There are rules of consideration."

"Maybe we should take this conversation away from here." He glanced at his tablemates. "No need to spoil their evening."

"If anyone has spoiled anything, I would say that it's you, Victor." She jutted out her lower lip. "I went to a lot of trouble for this evening, and you've done everything you could to ruin it for me."

Victor glanced at the onlookers at the table, then lowered his tone. "Look, I would rather keep this private . . . for your sake, but since you refuse, I might as well call it what it is. I never intended to bring you to the cotillion. I tried to tell you as much the other day, but you kept claiming I said something about this . . . probably months ago at the harvest party just because we danced a few times. But if you hadn't pressured me, or taken me on your guilt trip, I never would've brought you."

"I wish you hadn't!" she yelled.

His eyes widened but he kept his voice even. "Would you like me to take you home?"

"If that's not too much trouble for you," she seethed and, turning on her heel, she stormed off.

"Sorry, folks," he told the table. "This was fun, but her highness is ready to depart now."

Maria and Antonia chuckled, but Carol was too shocked to say anything. Larry was pleasantly oblivious, tapping his foot to the music, albeit slightly offbeat. After he was gone, Maria turned to Antonia. "Think he'll come back after he takes her home?"

"I hope so." Antonia frowned. "He was having such a good

time dancing." She made what seemed like a forced smile. "At least she didn't throw anything at you."

Maria laughed loudly now. "Yes, and I was getting ready to go hide the kitchen knives."

"Is she always like that?" Carol asked them.

"To be honest, I've never seen that side of her before," Antonia confessed, grimly shaking her head. "It was, well, a bit startling."

"I've heard she can get a bit upset when she doesn't get her way," Maria added.

Antonia turned to Maria. "She was obviously jealous of Carol."

Maria sighed. "I suppose we should've anticipated that. Too bad." Now the two of them began reminiscing about a similar incident many years ago with one of their female friends, and Carol noticed Larry was out of punch.

"More?" she asked, pointing to his cup.

"Yes." He nodded eagerly.

Glad for an excuse to escape the increasingly uncomfortable conversation, she returned to the refreshment table. She was just filling the cups when she heard two women talking in hushed tones. She couldn't be sure of what they were saying, but she recognized the voices from the bathroom and knew they were Victoria's friends, so she strongly suspected they were discussing her. *Well, let them*, she thought. Not much she could do about it anyway.

She strolled back slowly, pausing to take in the people who truly seemed to be enjoying the dance. It was such a pretty scene with the soft lighting and decor that she'd painstakingly set up. And the music and food were hits too. Perfect potential for a completely lovely evening. At least for some of them. She hoped so, anyway.

Back at the table, the older women were still exchanging stories about old friends and love triangles, so Carol did her best to engage with Larry. By now she knew to use only simple sentences with topics that didn't require a thought-out response from him. And he seemed to appreciate it.

Meanwhile, in the back of her mind, she wondered if Victor would return to the dance. She really hoped so, and she knew from something Antonia had said that Victoria lived in town. So it shouldn't take too long to drop her off and come back. But she also knew Victoria was adept at manipulation—and that she liked to get her way. It was possible she'd softened up by now, maybe even apologized . . . perhaps even enticed Victor into her house with food and drink. She might be trying to patch things up with him right now. Carol could imagine Victor, back in gentleman mode, even taking some of the blame. After all, he probably shouldn't have danced with Carol three times. What girl wouldn't feel a bit upset about that?

Not only that, but Victoria's pride was at stake here. Her girlfriends in the restroom already seemed to be planning the wedding—"third time's the charm," they'd said. "A diamond for Christmas." Maybe the queen and king of the cotillion had simply experienced a lovers' quarrel, a humorous story that the happy couple would laugh about in years to come, even regaling their tale to all their friends at their fiftieth anniversary.

Carol knew she was torturing herself with these thoughts, but she couldn't seem to stop them. Besides, maybe they were therapeutic. A way to get that man out of her system for good. Like her college friend Holly who'd told her a childhood story about how she'd been caught sneaking handfuls of her mom's Toll House cookies until her fed up mother told her to "have at it." So Holly gorged herself until she got sick as a dog, and after that day, swore off chocolate chip cookies forever.

Still feeling sick over her imaginings of Victor and Victoria, Carol made up her mind. As soon as she got back to Maria's, she would rebook her flight and go to the Bahamas after all. Sure, Maria would be disappointed, but really, she seemed greatly improved, and Antonia was nearby and willing to help. Perhaps she'd even invite Maria to come stay with them until she healed completely. Because, whatever it took, Carol felt—for the sake of her own mental health—she needed to get out of this place. Before Christmas!

14

As Carol helped a very tired Maria into her pajamas, she realized she couldn't hop on a plane and leave her like she'd imagined. Besides being selfish, it was cowardly and perhaps just plain stupid.

"Did you have a good evening?" Carol asked as she eased her into the bed.

"Yes. It was much better than I imagined possible." Maria fumbled to tug the quilt with her good arm.

Carol reached down to help arrange the covers. "I hope it didn't wear you out too much."

"I expect I'll sleep well." She gazed up at Carol. "You know what I enjoyed the most tonight?"

"No." Carol tucked the quilt under her aunt's chin, then straightened.

"Seeing you and Victor dancing." She smiled dreamily. "It was just beautiful."

"Uh-huh." Carol didn't really want to dwell on Victor.

"And I was so glad when he took Victoria home."

"Really?" Carol crossed her arms in front of her.

"You know he only took that girl to the cotillion out of obligation. But you can't expect a fellow to play the gentleman when he's being treated like that." She frowned. "I suspect tonight was the end of that relationship. And I say good riddance to Victoria."

"I wouldn't be too sure about that."

"What do you mean?"

Carol shrugged.

"Tell me why you're not so sure about that." Maria patted the bed and Carol reluctantly sat.

"Well, I, uh, overheard Victoria and her friends in the ladies' room."

Maria's eyes widened. "And?"

"One of her friends seemed to have inside information about an engagement ring that Victoria was going to receive for Christmas."

Maria laughed. "Well, that's nonsense."

"I don't know. She seemed pretty confident."

"But you saw the two of them bickering."

"Maybe that was just a lovers' quarrel. For all we know, they've made up by now." She fiddled with the quilt pattern. "That would explain why Victor didn't return to the cotillion."

"Oh . . ." Maria's brow creased. "I didn't think of that."

"Victoria is a very beautiful woman," Carol continued. "And I suspect when she wants to, she can be very sweet . . . and persuasive."

"Don't you mean manipulative?"

Carol shrugged again, then stood. "Well, I know you must be tired. I know I am."

"Victor is too smart to be manipulated by her," Maria declared.

Carol leaned down to kiss her aunt's cheek. "Well, I'm not going to worry about that tonight."

Maria's eyes flickered with interest. "So you do care?"

Carol forced a smile. "Victor is a nice guy. I'd hate to see him settle for the wrong woman."

Maria nodded. "Especially when the right woman might be waiting in the wings."

"Good night, Aunt Maria." Carol turned off the light. "Sweet dreams."

"You too, dear girl. I'm going to pray that your dream guy visits your dreams."

"Go ahead. Knock yourself out." Carol shook her head as she closed the door. Her aunt was one determined woman. As for being visited by her "dream guy," she seriously doubted it. As she got herself ready for bed, Carol did her best to block Victor from her thoughts, but as soon as she lay down, she remembered how fun it was to dance with him and how magical it felt to be in his arms. Despite her resolve, she had a feeling her aunt's prayers would be answered tonight.

* * * *

Right after breakfast the following morning, Maria insisted on deep cleaning her house. "Our Christmas Eve party is just two days out now," she told Carol, "and I always like to put the polish on the place."

"Can't we do that tomorrow?" Carol slid a plate into the dishwasher. It wasn't that she was tired herself, but she suspected Maria was still worn-out from last night.

"Tomorrow we'll go over and help Antonia get food ready for Christmas Eve. Then we bring half of it over here and Antonia brings the rest Christmas Eve. So our day will be full."

Carol didn't see how fixing food could take a whole day but assumed her aunt knew what she was talking about. "Well, I'll try my best to make your house sparkle and shine," she told her. "Just tell me what needs doing."

"The guest bathroom, for starters. It needs a thorough going-over."

"As soon as I get the breakfast things cleaned up, I'm on it."

All morning, Carol did her best to stay one step ahead of her aunt. By the time she had the bathroom spotless, she had no doubts that Maria was one of the most driven women she'd ever met. Even with one arm, she was a force to be reckoned with. But when Carol found her nearly toppling over as she used her good arm to sweep pine needles from the hardwood floor onto a dustpan she was balancing on one foot, she had to step in.

"Let me do that." She took the broom and handed Maria the dustrag. "Why don't you dust instead?"

"Yes, yes, I'm afraid I'm making more of a mess than anything. But I want to help. I feel so useless."

"I doubt anyone has ever considered you useless. Don't forget that yours is a temporary condition."

"I suppose you're right. But it does make me feel old. I hate feeling old."

They chattered back and forth as they worked together, but when Carol got out the vacuum cleaner, she encouraged Maria to sit down.

"But I haven't wiped the woodstove yet."

Carol took the dustrag from her and quickly wiped down the woodstove. "There. Now let me get the vacuuming done without having you underfoot." She pointed to Maria's favorite chair. "You need a break."

"Yes, I suspect I could use a little rest."

"Thank you." Carol smiled victoriously as she turned on the vacuum cleaner. She was just finishing up the area rug in the foyer when she thought she heard a phone ringing and then her aunt speaking loudly. Turning off the noisy machine, Carol listened. After a few seconds, she realized Maria was talking to her sister. Curious but not wanting to eavesdrop, she headed for the kitchen to make them both a cup of tea. As the kettle heated, she couldn't help but notice that Maria wasn't saying much, just the occasional "yes, uh-huh, I understand" peppered in here and there, which seemed to suggest that Mom was doing all the talking. Hopefully she wasn't being too hard on her sister.

Just as the kettle whistled, the phone conversation came to an end. Maria thanked Rosa for calling her. Then, as Carol poured hot water over the loose-leaf tea in the teapot, she heard Maria's footsteps behind her.

"Sounded like you were talking to my mom." She turned with a stiff smile, setting the teapot on the kitchen table. "So I thought we might both need a cup of tea."

"Tea and sympathy?" Maria sat down with a deflated sigh. "My sister . . . she can be a bit contrary."

Carol laughed as she set cups on the table.

"There's a tin of shortbread in the pantry," Maria told her. "I think I could use some."

"Good idea."

When they were both seated with tea and cookies, Carol asked her aunt if she wanted to talk about it.

Maria's eyes got teary. "Rosa must really think that I'm evil. She blames me for everything that's gone wrong in her life. And I agree that I wasn't a very good mother to her—"

"You weren't her mother though. You were a kid. You'd lost your mother too. My mom is so egocentric. Of course, she blames you. She can't take the responsibility for herself."

"Well, I'm to blame for that too. I never made her take responsibility as a child."

"But she's not a child now. Even if she acts like one. And think about it, Aunt Maria. Mom was a pretty pathetic mother to me growing up. And, well, I don't like to toot my own horn, but I didn't turn out too badly." She grimaced. "I hope."

Maria beamed at her. "You turned out perfectly."

"Well, I'm not sure I'd say perfect. But thanks."

Maria picked up a second cookie.

"Maybe the good news is that Mom wanted to talk to you," Carol added. "I assume she called you."

"She did." Maria sighed. "Caught me by surprise too."

"So, in her way, maybe she's trying." Carol sipped her tea.

"Maybe. And it might be my imagination, but I think she was a little more reasonable at the end of the conversation."

Probably not reasonable enough to apologize for her bad behavior. That would be too much to expect of Mom.

"I just hope the conversation was therapeutic for her. Perhaps it helped her to work through some things." Maria pursed her lips. "I'd like to think some good might come of it. For your mother, anyway."

"What Mom really needs is a good therapist." Carol snickered, then felt guilty. "I know I don't really understand her, but I've believed for some time that she's an honest-to-goodness narcissist. And based on what I've read, narcissists are hard to help, because they're so certain they're right and everyone else is wrong. Because of that, they seldom change. But it seems worth a try. Maybe I'll gently suggest she get some professional help." Then maybe she'll stop dumping her problems on everyone else.

"Or maybe we just need to be praying for her." Maria set down her empty teacup. "And forgiving her . . . and loving her . . . unconditionally."

Carol nodded but felt guilty as she gathered up the tea things. Was she honestly doing those things herself? She remembered how she'd once told her mother that refusing to forgive another was like eating poison and expecting the one you were angry with to get sick and die. Yet wasn't she withholding forgiveness from Mom?

Instead of dealing with her worries, she distracted herself with housework.

By the end of the day, the house was spotless, she was exhausted, and Maria was worn-out too. They both turned in early. But as Carol lay awake in her bed, she could no longer distract herself. She really did need to forgive her mom . . . before it ate her alive . . . or poisoned her. She knew she needed help to do this and so she prayed, honestly telling God that she felt powerless against her feelings. By the time she finished praying, she could tell something inside of her had changed. Oh, she might feel different by tomorrow and need to go through the whole process again, but for the moment, she felt that she'd forgiven her mother. She thanked God, took in a deep breath, and prepared herself for a good night's sleep.

15

Carol awoke refreshed and energized the next day. She looked out her window and soaked in the white snow sparkling in the sunlight and the wide span of clear blue sky. What a beautiful morning! She dressed warmly, then went downstairs to a quiet house and opened the drapes, letting the sunlight flow in. Seeing the darkened glass of the woodstove, she assumed her aunt would appreciate a fire, so she trekked outside. After sweeping off some of the blown snow from last night, she gathered a load of firewood and carried it in. She was cheerfully humming "Hark! The Herald Angels Sing" when Maria entered the room.

"Somebody's full of Christmas spirit this morning," her aunt said.

"How could I not be?" Carol smiled at her. "It's a beautiful day. We have a nice clean house. In a minute or two I'll have a nice fire going to take the chill off. And I'm about to make a pot of coffee."

"I'm not sure if you're an angel of mercy or one of Santa's elves, but I'm so glad you're here."

Carol lit the paper and kindling she'd arranged, then stood. "I'm so glad to be here." She thought about how close she'd come to abandoning her aunt just two days ago. "And you know what's caught me by surprise this morning?"

"What?"

"I'm actually looking forward to Christmas for the first time ever." Carol helped with the buttons on Maria's flannel shirt, impressed that she'd gotten this far dressed on her own.

"Wonderful. I'm looking forward to it too." Maria sighed. "I didn't expect to feel like that . . . ever again."

Carol hugged her aunt. "I'm sure you'll have your sad moments. It's only natural."

"Yes. I've heard the first Christmas after losing a loved one can be hard. But with you here to help me face it, I feel hopeful." She glanced toward the kitchen. "Now how about that coffee?"

"Coming right up."

* * * *

After breakfast, Carol drove Maria to the Clarksons', which was just down the road. Their house looked newer, though it had a very similar feel to Maria's property. As she helped Maria out of the car and onto the porch, Carol felt a slight wave of trepidation wash over her. She was on Victor's turf, and bumping into him seemed inevitable. Maria had mentioned he was probably out doing chores. She must've suspected Carol's uneasiness. Although, she couldn't know why Carol had anxiety about seeing him.

Antonia greeted them at the door and welcomed them inside. Their house was warm and homey but not nearly as carefully put together as Maria's home. Still, it was cozy.

Larry waved from his recliner and Carol went over to say hello while Antonia helped Maria remove her coat.

"You don't have to stay here and work in the kitchen if you have other things you need to be doing," Antonia told Carol.

"I don't have anything that needs doing." She smiled. "But I could visit with Larry a bit."

Antonia's expression relayed how much that would be appreciated. So as the older women headed for the kitchen, Carol sat down to chat with Larry. She made small talk that he may or may not have understood, but he seemed grateful for the attention. Larry looked half asleep when she was finally running out of topics of conversation. She heard the front door open and turned to see Victor coming in. Holding a forefinger to her lips, she tipped her head toward his dad. Victor motioned for her to come over to him.

"Want to do some errands in town with me?" he whispered.

"Sure." She nodded nervously.

"Get your coat and I'll let my mom know."

* * * *

Carol was surprised how good it felt to be riding next to him in his pickup . . . again. Like coming home, although that made no sense. She was still a bit nervous, but at the same time she felt relaxed. That, too, made no sense.

"Isn't it a beautiful day?" she asked, mostly to break the silence.

"For sure." He nodded. "I, uh, I wanted to talk to you yesterday, but I guess I got pretty busy with farm chores."

"We were busy too." She briefly described Maria's deep-cleaning binge.

"I wanted to apologize to you—for what happened at the cotillion."

"Apologize?" She turned to stare at him. "For what?"

"For the way I treated Victoria mostly. Especially in front of my parents and Maria and you. I should've handled it differently, but I was so fed up, I guess I wasn't thinking clearly."

"You did seem frustrated."

"Well, I got hornswoggled into taking her."

"Now there's a word you don't hear too often." She chuckled.

"It pretty much describes what happened. I honestly don't

recall giving her my word that I'd take her, but she was convinced, so I thought I'd just get it over with and go. I didn't realize that she'd want to keep me on a leash at the dance. Or that she'd throw a hissy fit if I danced with someone else."

"Did you get it all ironed out with her?"

"I don't know. Mostly I wanted her to understand that she and I are not a thing. We never have been." He glanced at Carol. "I wanted you to know that too."

Carol felt a little flutter inside but didn't know how to respond.

"I'm not sure she understood," he continued. "Or maybe she didn't want to understand. When she finally went into her house, I'm pretty sure she was still mad." He shrugged. "But that's her choice."

"Well, thanks for telling me." Carol felt like an invisible weight had been lifted from her. She almost confessed about how, in the ladies' room, she'd overheard talk about diamonds and things. But she didn't want to frustrate him further. "I'll admit I did wonder . . . you know, about the status of your relationship."

"There is no relationship," he declared. "I used to think she was a friend, but now I wouldn't even claim that. My folks are sure relieved. I bet Maria will be too. She's lectured me before. Guess I should've listened." He chuckled. "You live and learn I guess."

For the rest of the drive into town, they just visited like old friends. And it felt good. First off, they picked up a few ingredients at the grocery store. Then a prescription from the drugstore for Larry. While Victor waited on that, Carol browsed, hoping to find something Maria might like for Christmas. Of course, nothing seemed quite right, but she went ahead and got a few items. A pretty cinnamon-and-spice candle, a box of yummy-looking chocolates, and some luxurious skin products. She'd noticed some baskets in Maria's attic and planned to borrow one to make these offerings more festive. She was just trying to find a Christmas card when Victor joined her.

"I wanted something special for Maria," she explained. "Not that I've had much luck. I'm almost done."

"No rush." He began perusing the cards too, contentedly humming along with the Christmas music bubbling out of the sound system. And it didn't even aggravate her. Before long, they had paid for their purchases and were back in the pickup.

"My errands in town are done," he told her. "But if you have time, I want to stop by and look at something."

"I have all the time in the world."

"Great." He pointed to a large building just a couple blocks down the street. "My buddy Jason is a realtor, and he gave me a key to his place."

"What is it?" She stared at the rather boxy-looking, neglected building.

"It's the old grain mill. And it's for sale."

"For sale?" She felt her brows arch. "And you're in the market for a ginormous building like that?"

He laughed as he drove over. "Maybe. Especially when the price is right."

A sign with peeling paint, hanging crookedly in front, read "Crafter's Mall."

"Are you planning to sell crafts?" She asked as he unlocked the door.

"Now that would be a surefire way to lose money considering I'm all thumbs when it comes to arts and crafts."

"What then?"

"Well . . ." He let the door swing open. "I am good at restaurants."

She stepped inside and looked around. "In this big barn of a building?"

"Oh, come on," he urged. "I thought your creative brain might kick into gear. Whatever happened to country chic?"

She had to laugh at herself. "I'm sorry. Let me regroup here. I'll put on my designer's cap." She closed her eyes, took a breath, then opened them. "Wow. Okay, I think I can see it."

"Seriously?" He blinked.

"Well, the space is probably too big as it is. No one wants to eat in a barn. But what if you separated it? You know, break it up some. A restaurant over there." She pointed to one side. "A lounge there, maybe with a small music stage. And what about a shop near the door for specialty food items? You know, like some of the things you use in your restaurant? Maybe you could even lease it out to someone to help cover expenses."

Victor was nodding eagerly. "Yes, yes, and yes. Wow, you really do have a designer's brain."

"And you're right about keeping the decor country chic. But you'd want it to be Italian country chic. I'm thinking Tuscany. Like an old mill building in the Tuscan hill country. Maybe a winery or olive oil factory. Not that I've been there to see any of that. But I've read some fabulous books." She listed several titles. "And the authors wrote as much about decor as food. It felt like I was really there. In fact, I've dreamed of going there ever since reading those."

"But you chose the Bahamas?" he asked.

"Well, that's because I was alone, and it was a good deal. I think you really need someone to go with you to a place like Tuscany." She didn't admit she'd dreamt of a Tuscan honeymoon.

"I love your ideas," he told her. "Is this a free consultation, or are you going to send me a bill?"

She laughed, but continued strolling about the building's interior, listing its assets, like the plank floors and bulky posts and beams that were probably a hundred years old. "It's really a diamond in the rough," she finally proclaimed. "Well, as long as you can afford it . . . and afford to fix it up. The suggestions I'm making would be pretty costly."

"All good points." He rubbed his chin. "And I'll admit that originally I was just curious about the potential here. I hadn't really dreamed that it could possibly happen." He turned to look at her. "I think I've been thinking more about dreams . . . ever since that time we talked about it. It's like something ignited in me."

She just nodded. "I've sort of felt the same. I think we need to nurture our dreams."

"And seize the moment," he said. "It's one thing to just dream about something but another thing to act on it."

"Do you really think you might buy this place?" She felt a smidgen of worry now. Hopefully she wasn't encouraging him to board a sinking ship.

"I'm going to carefully consider it. And, of course, I need to pray about it as well. This time, I'd like God to be directing me."

She was relieved. "Good for you."

He looked at his watch. "It's past noon. You hungry?"

"I could be."

"Well, I'm starved. I had a bowl of dry cereal before dawn so I could finish up my chores early. And if you can trust me, I have a plan. Something I hope you'll enjoy."

"Try me."

He grinned. "Okay. I'm going to assume you're an outdoorsy girl."

"I used to be . . . before my work got so demanding. Then time sort of got away from me. But I used to hike and bike and ski and all sorts of things."

"Ski?" His eyes lit up. "How about snowshoeing?"

"I've always wanted to try it, but—"

"Fantastic. Let me make some quick phone calls."

Within mere minutes, Victor had gotten them a brown bag lunch from the deli to take with them, and they were outfitted for snowshoeing. Carol knew such accomplishments would've taken hours in Seattle. But in a tiny town like this, where Victor seemed to know everyone, it was all surprisingly simple.

It took less than thirty minutes to get to a small wildlife preserve outside Miller's Creek. As they tromped around on virgin snow, the world became a magical place. But Carol felt the best part was just being with Victor. He was so much fun, and when she stumbled, he would gently pull her back to her feet. On her third or fourth fall, he pulled her up and then held her so close, she could feel his heart thumping in his chest. Or was it hers?

He was looking right into her eyes with an intensity that took her breath away. And it wasn't just from snowshoeing either! And just like that, it happened—he kissed her. Gently and tenderly at first, but then, as she responded, he added so much passion that she felt slightly dizzy when he let her go and stepped back. So much so that she lost her balance and her feet—like a clown with oversized shoes—flew up in the air as she fell backward. He reached out to stop her fall, but instead of catching her, he tumbled down in a heap of poles and snowshoes and flying snow as well. Both were laughing so hard, they could barely get back up on their feet. Almost like a real icebreaker, they were now so jovial and happy and comfortable that the trek back to the pickup felt like a short hop.

Despite the sun being swallowed by heavy-laden clouds, Carol thought this had been the happiest afternoon ever. And not just because of the amazing kisses either. Trekking across snowfields, pausing by sparkling streams fringed with snow and ice, taking a lunch break on a brushed-off bench next to a shimmering frozen lake, she knew these were memories that would be fixed in her head—and her heart—until she was a very old lady. As they unloaded their gear into the back of the pickup, they were both flushed and winded and immensely happy.

"You did great," he told her after they got inside the cab. "What a trouper."

"I loved it. Absolutely amazing," Carol said as Victor started driving home. "I totally love snowshoeing. It's even better than skiing. You go so fast on skis that you miss a lot of the beauty all around you. And I never realized a snowscape could be so beautiful."

"You get much snow near Seattle?"

"Mostly rain," she admitted.

"For a girl who seems to enjoy snow and winter activities, you might want to think about relocating," he said, giving her a quick wink.

She knew it wouldn't take much to budge her out of Seattle right now. Like the perfect man, for instance . . . but she had no intention of revealing that kind of vulnerability to him just yet. Good grief, the poor guy already had one woman chasing after him with marriage on the mind. He'd probably head for the hills if he thought there were two. Even if he wasn't interested in Victoria, her pursuits had definitely put him off. And for all Carol knew, Victoria's pursuits were not over.

As if to confirm her theory, Carol noticed a shiny red SUV parked in front of the Clarkson house, with Victoria standing next to it, smiling and waving. Unlike Carol's odd ensemble of borrowed clothing, Victoria's outfit looked like it belonged on the cover of a trendy winter sportswear catalogue.

"Looks like you have a visitor," she said quietly.

His response was a low groan. "This should be interesting."

"Yeah. I bet. I think I'll scoot on into the house. It's already starting to snow and I'm, uh, kinda cold."

"Good idea. Avoid some of the screaming."

Studying Victoria's face as she climbed out of the pickup, Carol suspected he could be right. Victoria's happy countenance evaporated. Clearly the queen was angry. Probably more so at Carol than Victor. Just the same, Carol forced a smile and threw out a cheerful greeting, then she excused herself and hurried toward the house.

She risked looking back and noticed Victoria's greeting was icier than the wind that was starting to blow, and on her face was a frozen smile, with eyes fixed on Victor. "Oh, Vic," she exclaimed. "I'm so glad to find you here. I have to tell you how sorry I am about the cotillion. I was so horrid to you. Truly awful! It's been eating me alive for two days now. I hope you can forgive me. Give me a second chance." Her voice literally quivered with emotion. Was this real? Or manufactured?

Eager to escape what promised to be a heartbreaking melodrama, at least for Victoria, Carol opened the front door. What was Victoria trying to pull off here? Did she think she could turn Victor's head with tears? But one last glance at Victor made Carol wonder if perhaps that's exactly what was happening. The poor man looked totally blindsided by the beautiful blond in his driveway. Was it because Victoria didn't normally apologize? Or because he thought she truly deserved a second chance? Or was it that they had a history . . . because Victoria was the hometown, homegrown girl and reigning queen of Miller's Creek?

Carol went inside and spotted Antonia and Maria spying out the front window, taking in the spectacle unfolding outside. Carol stood behind the two women, watching as well. Carol noticed that Victoria had what looked like real tears streaming down her cheeks. With her arms spread, she ran to Victor, throwing herself against his chest. He looked shocked and speechless and finally pointed to her vehicle. She nodded and hurried over but got in the passenger's seat. Victor looked flustered, but finally he ran around and jumped into the driver's side. With the tinted windows, the show was over.

"Well, what do you make of that?" Antonia said to no one in particular.

"I'm guessing that's a first," Maria admitted. "For Victoria, anyway."

Antonia frowned. "What do you think she's up to?"

"Obviously, she's trying to hold on to him. And why not?" Maria shook her head. "That boy is a great catch. For the right woman."

"I don't think Victoria's the right woman." Antonia peeked out again, then sighed deeply. "Although her money is probably tempting. I heard she's got a couple million stashed away from her first two marriages. And I know Victor wants to start another restaurant."

"Oh, Antonia." Maria tsked. "You know your son better than that."

"What do you make of it?" Antonia asked Carol.

She just shrugged. Quite honestly, she had no words. She looked out the window just in time to see the SUV driving away.

"Well, never mind that," Maria said. "He's probably just trying to get that hysterical girl out of here. More power to him."

Antonia turned to Carol. "Anyway, you're back just in time. We're all done, and I've loaded some things for tomorrow in the back of Maria's car. But I'm sure she's all tuckered out. Time to get home and rest up for tomorrow's festivities."

Carol nodded mutely. Soon she was helping Maria down the slippery porch stairs, through the blowing snow, and into the car, and without saying a word, she drove them both home.

By the time Carol got Maria to bed, she realized her cell phone was dead again. Being out here in the country had lessened the need to be hyperconnected. Instead of charging it, she took a relaxing bath. She didn't want Mom to call and doubted that Victor would bother this late. She could sort this all out tomorrow. Tonight she was tired. And really, she told herself, Victor cared more for her than Victoria. Didn't he? She wondered about his restaurant dream and how much money that would take . . . She knew Victoria was wealthy. What if she offered to fund it? But she didn't think Victor was the kind of guy who could be bought! Right?

Carol and Maria had plenty to keep them busy on Christmas Eve day. And even though Carol's phone was charged now, Victor hadn't called. Her mom did though. She was surprisingly civil, only calling to wish Carol a merry Christmas. Carol was careful to keep their conversation light and upbeat. But to her surprise, Mom told her to wish Maria a merry Christmas too.

"How about if she calls you tomorrow?" Carol had suggested cautiously. "We're having people over today so she's pretty busy." Mom agreed that would be nice and after they said goodbye, Carol resisted the urge to pinch herself and even double-checked her caller ID to confirm that she really had been talking to her mother. Not wanting to give Maria false hopes for reuniting with her baby sister, she decided to keep the contents of that call under wraps until tomorrow.

Everything was set with about an hour to spare before guests were to arrive when someone knocked on the front door. Since Maria was relaxing with a cup of tea, Carol jumped up to get it. To her surprise and pleasure, it was Victor. In his hand was a giant ball of mistletoe. He grinned.

"Know what this is?" he asked with a twinkle in his dark eyes.

She nodded primly. "I believe I do."

Now he held it in the air between them. "Mind if I put it to use?"

She held up one finger to stop him. "I don't mind at all, but how about we clear the air some first? Then I'll enjoy the mistletoe more."

He lowered his arm and looked down. "Victoria?"

She nodded again, waiting for his explanation.

"Well, I *had* to take her home yesterday. Man, was she a hot mess! I was afraid if she drove herself to town, she'd wind up in a ditch or wrapped around a tree."

"Yes, I can understand that." She felt her spirits lightening.

"Then I got my buddy Graydon to give me a ride back home."

"And that's it?"

He shrugged. "Well, I thought I'd already made myself clear with her on cotillion night. Actually even before that. I mean, I laid my cards on the table last fall. I could never be serious about her. But yesterday I had to spell it all out." He seemed a bit sheepish. "And you'll have to forgive me . . . I may have used your name a bit out of context."

"*Used* my name?"

"Well, Victoria doesn't take no for an answer, Carol. She's used to getting her own way."

Carol stepped closer to him, softening. "Uh-huh?"

"I, uh, I told her that if I was going to be involved with anyone, well, it would be someone like you." He half smiled. "Someone *exactly* like you."

Now she reached over to take his hand, then moved the mistletoe up above her head, tilting her face toward him. He chuckled, then rewarded her with a tender kiss.

"Goodness, children!" Maria scolded from behind Carol. "Come inside the house and close that door. It's like the North Pole out there. I don't mind if Santa shows up, but I don't want him and all the reindeer stomping into my house."

They all laughed and went inside.

The Christmas Eve celebration was the most wonderful gathering Carol had ever attended. All the friends and neighbors felt strangely familiar to her, as if she'd known them her whole life. And Victor, sweetly attentive, didn't hide his feelings for Carol around any of them. Maybe that was why they accepted her so readily.

They ate amazing food, sang carols, toasted with eggnog and yuletide drinks, and when it was all said and done, Carol knew she'd never experienced a Christmas like this. After the guests had left, Victor remained to assist with cleanup while Carol helped Maria get ready for bed.

"So what do you think of Christmas now?" Maria asked just as Carol was about to turn off the bedside lamp.

"I think if I died tonight, I would die completely happy."

"Good grief, don't do that. Tomorrow is your birthday, not to mention Christmas Day. We're only half done." Maria patted Carol's cheek. "Besides, poor Victor would be devastated."

"Don't worry. I plan to stick around." Carol kissed her aunt good night, turned off the light, and went out to find Victor, who was just putting the last dish into the dishwasher.

"Looks like you got it all cleaned up already," she said.

"Didn't I tell you I'm handy in the kitchen?" he teased. "A good guy to keep around."

"Not to mention the fact that the foods you and your mom fixed tonight were amazing." She patted her midsection. "I'm still stuffed."

"Well, we have something even more special on the menu for tomorrow. But it'll be a much smaller gathering. Just my parents and me . . . and Maria and you, if you can work up an appetite by then."

"I'll be there with bells on."

"I'd like to see that." He chuckled as he took her hand and led her to the foyer, right under the spot where he'd hung the

167

mistletoe from the chandelier. "Let's seal the deal." He gently drew her toward him . . . and kissed her. "See you tomorrow, darling."

* * * *

Carol could tell that Maria was still a little worn-out the next morning. "I think we should both take it easy today," she told her as she cleared their breakfast plates.

"My thoughts exactly." Maria sighed happily. "We had such a lovely evening yesterday."

"I couldn't agree more. And in case I didn't tell you, I love Christmas now. I think what was missing was family and friends." She grinned as she refilled their coffee mugs. "And really good food!"

"A recipe for success." Maria tipped her head to one side. "I don't want to pressure you for information, Carol, but I couldn't help but notice that you and Victor seem to have hit it off."

Carol smiled. Or maybe she beamed, she couldn't really tell. All she knew was she was happier than before. Happier than ever. She told Maria how Victor had straightened her out about Victoria. "He even explained that his friend Jason never would've told anyone they were about to become engaged."

"I knew it," Maria declared. "I just knew it. She was all wrong for him."

"I agree."

"And you are all right." Maria winked.

Carol nodded, still smiling.

"Except for one thing."

"What?"

Maria frowned. "You live on the other side of the country."

Carol bit her lip, remembering that Marsha expected her back in a couple of days. "That's true."

"Do you really want to go back to Seattle?"

Carol looked down at her coffee, swirling it around in the mug and thinking. "The honest truth is I don't care if I do or I don't."

"Do you think you could ever be happy living here in Michigan? In a small town like this?"

Carol looked up. "Under the right circumstances, yes, I think I could. It's hard to explain, but something about this place has felt more like home than any place I've ever known."

Maria's whole face lit up. "Well, you know you are welcome to stay here with me. Indefinitely."

"Thanks." Carol felt her head spinning slightly. Would she really consider staying? Seriously? She thought about her stark, modern apartment and all the rainy days in Seattle. It didn't even compare. And yet . . . how did one make a huge life change like that?

Her thoughts were interrupted by the sound of a phone ringing. It was the landline, and Maria was already up getting it. Carol could tell by Maria's responses that it was Mom. But Maria didn't sound stressed like before. In fact, she sounded almost pleased.

"Well, that's really nice of you, Rosa. I wish you and Ed a merry Christmas too." Maria paused to listen. "Oh, I would love that, dear. Come anytime. You are always welcome." Another pause. "Yes, I'll tell her. I love you, Rosa. Have a good day." She hung up and turned to Carol with glistening eyes. "A miracle has begun."

Carol went over to hug her. "I know. Mom called me yesterday too. She sounded different."

"She wants to come visit. Maybe as soon as New Year's. Can you believe it?"

Carol wanted to say no but nodded her head just the same. "That'd be amazing."

"I'm going to go rest some," Maria told her. "I want to be ready for Christmas at the Clarksons'." She blinked in surprise.

"Oh, yes, happy birthday, Carol. I completely forgot, but your mother said to tell you happy birthday."

* * * *

Dinner at the Clarksons' was an incredible feast of stracciatella soup and cannelloni, some amazing red wine, and several other delectable dishes Carol had never tasted and couldn't even pronounce. The meal was followed by coffee and panforte, a delicious cake made by Antonia, which was lit with candles and accompanied with the singing of the birthday song.

"This is all so sweet," Carol told them. "Thank you."

"That's not all." Maria came out with a couple of wrapped presents. "These are for you too."

"I don't know what to say." Carol felt close to tears. "I've never had a birthday like this before." She took her time to open her gifts. Antonia and Larry gave her a beautiful shawl that was handmade by Antonia.

"That'll keep you warm on a cold winter's night," Maria told her. "In case you don't have a strong set of arms to hold you." Everyone laughed.

From Maria she got a beautiful cameo brooch. "It was from Don's grandmother," her aunt explained. "I always wanted to give it to a daughter, and you're the closest thing."

"It looks Italian," Antonia said as she examined it. "Yes, now I remember. Don once told me that his maternal grandma came from the same region as my family. Somewhere near Florence."

Maria dropped her jaw. "I must've forgotten that."

"It's beautiful." Carol hugged her aunt. "Thank you."

"I wore it on my wedding gown." Maria pulled back with a sparkle in her eyes.

"Right." Carol tucked the lovely brooch back into the box.

"Okay, this isn't much," Victor told her, "but I was kinda distracted yesterday, and I never had time to go out and shop for anything." He held out a rolled-up blue T-shirt that didn't look exactly new. He wore a lopsided grin as the shirt unrolled to reveal an outline of his home state, shaped like a mitten, and words that read "I love Michigan." "This was my favorite shirt in high school."

"I will treasure it always." She held the soft T-shirt close to her, resisting the urge to sniff it.

"And this"—he handed her a card—"I actually swiped from Mom's stash." Carol smiled as she removed it from the envelope to see a Christmas card. He'd used a felt pen to add "Happy Birthday" to the front. Inside was a typical Christmas greeting, along with his own words.

Follow your dreams, Carol. But please don't go back to Seattle. Home is where the heart is. Give Michigan (and me) a chance. I think we can make you happy.

Love, Victor

Still holding the beloved T-shirt and card, she jumped up and threw her arms around Victor. "You're right. And I think my heart has found its home. As of now, I'm not going anywhere." The others around the table clapped and cheered, and Victor held her tight, like he never planned to let go. And she didn't either. They sealed the moment with a kiss.

Melody Carlson is the award-winning author of more than 250 books with sales of more than 7.5 million, including many bestselling Christmas novellas, young adult titles, and contemporary romances. She received a *Romantic Times* Career Achievement Award, her novel *All Summer Long* has been made into a Hallmark movie, and the movie based on her novel *The Happy Camper* premiered on UPtv in 2023. She and her family live in central Oregon.

MEET
Melody

f MelodyCarlsonAuthor
@ AuthorMelodyCarlson